# MENTORING WRITERS SHORT STORY BOOK

## By

## Assorted Authors

Copyright Written Work: © Assorted Authors
as Shown 2021
Copyright Images: © Ann Brady 2021

Publisher: Pen & Ink Designs 2021

ISBN: 978-1-915086-02-0

# "MENTORING WRITERS" COMPETITION WINNERS 2021

All the stories in this book were written by new, developing, and established authors who entered our Summer 2021 Writing Competition.

The entrants were allowed to write a story in any genre. The entrants were wide and varied and of an exceptionally high quality which made judging harder this year.

The stories published in this book have been chosen by our panel of independent judges as being the '**best of the best**.' Each Judge has given their opinion on each story.

We congratulate all those included in this year's book and commiserate with those who didn't quite make it.

To our readers, we hope you enjoy all the stories as much as our judges did.

**www.mentoringwriters.co.uk**

# CONTENTS

# THE HEART-SHAPED CARVING IN THE OLD OAK TREE

## By MASON BUSHELL

## Genre - Romance

A walk in the woods; a regular event for a person and their dog. Just the whistle of the breeze through the limbs of the oaks, silver birch, and the yew trees can lower the blood pressure. Just the feeling of nature all around, hugging you can make you relax. The twittering and tweeting of the many birds. The squirrel watching from above with an acorn in his paws. The knocking of a woodpecker, searching for grubs. And that majestic deer peeking around the gnarled old trunk of a tree. All these wondrous sights and sounds make wandering in the woods a special thing to do. Even if you've been a hundred times, it's still a great experience. A new creature, an odd mushroom, or a new sunny space make it all worthwhile. There's never really an adventure unless you miss your way.

That's what Megan did one afternoon, whilst out with her black German Sheppard Lucy. Megan was twenty-three and had tawny brown hair that glinted in the sun. Its warm rays gracing her bare shoulders as it passed, dappled, through the canopy of the leaves above. Lucy snuffling about the bracken for something to chase, and chaffinches fluttering about with the butterflies. There was tranquillity there in the woods. Megan stopped and breathed, opened her arms in a beam of sunlight, then turned energizing circles. The skirts of her cream skater dress flared as wide as her relaxed smile. So calm was she walking in the woods, that a mistake she made.

When the young lady stopped turning she walked on in quite the wrong direction. Lucy noticed and lowered an ear. 'No, my mistress knows where she's going,' she thought, before trotting obediently after her. One rabbit path is quite like another when in amongst the trees. Megan walked between holly bushes, around birches and a cherry tree on the path that led the wrong way. Suddenly the rabbit path was gone and a glade surrounded by silver birches was at its end. Open to the blue sky and welcoming it was. Wildflowers, dog roses, honeysuckle and violets filled the woodland floor. Between them, delicate bracken ferns and the mysterious enchanter's nightshade grew.

Lucy dog arrived first. She stood one front paw aloft, confused, alarmed even by the strange new place. Megan felt it too. There was an energy here and it was all in the oak tree. It stood centre to and toward the back of the clearing. Its display of enormous limbs fanned out like the spans of a cathedral's magnificent roof. Each gnarled and weathered yet as beautiful as could be. The tree was a thousand years old if it was a day. The squirrels adored it, this was their home, as did the colourful jay.

Megan approached, her head tilted high. She loved the light trickling through the massive, magnificent canopy. The oak seemed to draw her in, it's feeling warm and enchanting. Megan arrived at the trunk and stepped over a raised root. Her sandals allowed her white, painted toes to touch the wood that supplied the tree with nutrients from the ground. It felt alive with energy, but not as much as the cankerous, gnarly trunk. It was warm from the sun and felt happy to be growing there in the woods. Happier still to feel Megan's pure, friendly touch.

"What a magnificent tree, hey, Lucy. I feel something magical happened here," Megan said. Even as she did, she felt she was on the wrong side of the wide trunk. Lucy still hadn't come closer, preferring the edge of glade to the tree that set her senses on alert. Megan smiled at her then worked her way around the massive girth of the oak. A squirrel above chattered, beckoned her upwards. Higher still, a spotted woodpecker watched on with interest. Reaching the other side, she stumbled on a root, dropping to a knee. Unhurt she rose again and saw the proof of an event. There above the first branches, it was, a heart carved into the tree. There was lettering inside, worn with age, but indecipherable from the floor. Megan kicked off her sandals and smoothed her hair over her shoulder.

"Don't go anywhere, Lucy, I need to see," she said before beginning to climb. With bare toes, hands, legs, and arms, she could feel every crack in the bark, every wrinkle that had shown its time on earth. Then she was sat on the branch, with the squirrel still on a branch not far away. A stag beetle stood by a hole higher up; the home of owls or bats perhaps. Megan knew the humble oak tree was home to a multitude of creatures. Important to many more for food and protection too. Her soft brown eyes moved to the heart. Now it was clear. True love was professed right here. '*E. W. & G. F.*' it read. The ampersand wasn't there, just two entwined circlets filling the space.

"I see you experienced beautiful love, didn't you, tree?" Megan reached out and placed her finger on the heart, she traced the letters within. As she finished the 'W' her branch perch began to wobble. The shudder felt from within. It shook her against the trunk. Her palm pressed flat upon the heart and her consciousness faded to green.

When next she could see, Megan was still in the tree. On the same branch but away from the trunk. No heart or initials showed in the bark. The leaves sparkled with browns and yellows, it was autumn in the woods. A smooth honey-brown doe was grazing below, and Lucy dog was gone. Footsteps were coming. Megan glanced about the woods below her. Where were they? Who were they? Then she saw her, a young lady close to her age, yet in a style much older. She was wearing a loose-fitting, drop waist, cream dress. A blue cloche hat sat upon her bob of short brown hair. Accessorised by Mary Jane shoes and a beaded bag, she was a girl from yesteryear. Megan loved fashion, so she knew this girl was, by her dress from the 1920s, no less. By the tears in her eyes, she was definitely in distress. Megan tried to descend the tree, to help if she could. She couldn't move, not an inch of her would react to her desire to get out of the oak tree. It was as if it held her in its leafy embrace and would hold her until it permitted her to leave.

"Elsie, wait!" The call was from a young man, for now out of sight. There had been an 'E' engraved in the tree before, not now there. Was this her? Megan had no choice but to look on with interest. Elsie wiped away a tear and walked on. Stopping there under the tree.

"No, Geoff, I demand you leave me be," she said with tears in her eyes.

There he was coming around the last silver birch tree. A handsome gentleman, not much less than twenty. He strode into the glade wearing black trousers, over Oxford-style two-tone blue and white shoes. The blue was picked up in his matching boater blazer, with underneath a crisp white shirt. A white boater hat with a blue band finished his 1920s college boy look.

"I cannot, Elsie. I made a big mistake. Will you give me a chance to explain," he pleaded. Then he was stood next to Elsie beneath the tree. He made to put his arm about her, but she shrugged him away.

"I told you, Geoff, leave me be. I saw you kissing Mary-Jane. Is my sister prettier than me?" she cried having placed her head on her hand, against the oak tree. From above, Megan could see, she was sobbing.

"I don't deny it, I did kiss Mary-Jane, but not for her beauty and not for love. In fact, I kissed her for something she did for me. Something special, so I could do properly by you. She'll never be prettier, and I'll never love her over you. Will you let me show you what your sister did for you?" Geoff requested.

With exception to the birds and breeze within the woods, silence fell in the glade. Nearly a minute passed as Geoff waited for Elsie to answer, hoping to be permitted one last chance.

"You kissed my sister, something you should never do. You say you still love me. Maybe I can't love you now," she said at last. On the bough above Megan felt sad at what she saw, what she heard, from the couple beneath the tree.

"Go on, Elsie. Give him a chance. I'm sure he meant well and will see you happy again, very soon." she said aloud. Neither Elsie nor Geoff looked up. They couldn't see her, couldn't hear her or so it seemed.

"Dear sweet, Elsie. The kiss was a thank you and nothing more. Turn to face me and you'll see. She helped me get this to give to you with my heart." Geoff tried again. It was then the squirrel climbed from the tree. The creature graced Elsie's shoulder then bounded to her feet. To follow it she turned looking toward Geoff. The Squirrel gave a chunter, a bow, and to the tree, it returned. The gentleman held a black heart-shaped box. He opened it, revealing a ruby ring sitting within.

"Why do you have that, Geoff?" she asked, interested now.

"One day in twenty-one, you told me of a ring you and Mary-Jane loved. It was for that ring she earned her kiss. You see, she led me to it that day. Now I hold it before you as a token of love. Dear, Elsie. My heart and soul are yours, may yours be mine. Will you marry me, my love?" Geoff dropped to a knee. Above him, Megan shed a tear that fell upon the branch of the tree. The oak tree had indeed played witness to a moment of pure love.

Elsie wiped her eyes and looked at Geoff. "You mean the kiss was to get me this, all along?" she asked.

"It was, dear, Elsie. It's you I love, and I always will. Will you let me take care of you?" and Geoff offered the ring in its box; his heart on the sleeve of his outstretched hand. Elsie's smile all but lit up the glade, even the birds seemed to cheer.

"Yes, Geoff, I will. I will marry you," she said. Bounding to his feet, whereupon he placed the ring on her finger and the two shared a kiss. Her back against the trunk, his lips glued to hers, their love flowed again. Although they didn't know, it flowed into and imbuing the silently smiling oak tree.

Megan beamed at the couple and winked at the squirrel. He was back watching from a branch not too far away. Then Elsie broke from the kiss.

"Darling, Geoff. We must do something to help us remember this moment," she said while straightening the cloche hat on her head. The young man looked up with a grin and a nod.

"I know what to do," he said. "Let's climb up there."

"Not in this dress, besides no lady can climb up the tree." Elsie disagreed.

Geoff leant a knee and offered a hand. "Sure you can, up you go. It's easy, you'll see." And the young man gave an encouraging nod with an enchanting smile.

This time Elsie stepped forward and up she went. Within moments she was perched on the branch. Sitting where Megan was now. Never touching, never seeing, yet sharing the same space, but in a different time. Geoff was with her in no time at all. From his belt, he took a small knife and began to carve into the trunk with a deft hand.

"What are you doing?" she asked as the heart took shape. Megan smiled, she had seen what was to come. Seen what was to be carved into the oak tree.

"I'm carving our moment into the tree. A mark to remember our time together, forever." Geoff finished the heart. Then wrapping Elsie's soft hand on the knife he began on the letters. "E, W for Elsie White and G, F for Geoff Flynn," he said as they carved the initials. Her hands-free again, Elsie watched as he carved in the circlets.

"And two entwined rings for our love. Our marriage is to happen very soon," she said. With the carving complete he turned her back to the tree trunk and kissed her again. Her hat fell to the ground. Their clothes, Megan felt sure were to follow. Their love grew and grew, and it was blessed by the tree. Then as Megan grew hot under the collar, Elsie's hand pressed the carving and the scene faded to green once more.

Megan's eyes flickered open, she was still in the tree. A barking below, let her know Lucy was back and so was she. Wasting no time she climbed down from the tree. "You know, Lucy. It's time to go now the tree's taken its magic from me," she remarked.

With a look over her shoulder at the old oak tree, she saw across the glade there was an elderly couple, joined at the hand and hearts as well. She wearing an old red dress, and he a casual grey suit. On her finger was a ruby, a familiar engagement ring. With it was a wedding band to match the one upon the finger of the gentleman.

"Not many people find their way to our special oak tree," said the lady as she and the gentleman on his black cane stepped forward. Megan felt stunned, could they be them from so long ago?

"Good afternoon, I'm Megan and this is Lucy dog. Are you Elsie White and Geoff Flynn?" she asked, even though she already knew they were.

"That is indeed us. Do we know you?" Geoff asked. A twinkle in his eye told more than his words.

Megan shook her head. "No, I saw your carving. The tree showed me the rest. The day when you proposed to Elsie here in the glade. After Mary-Jane got that ring and that risky kiss. Please, how did I see that day so long ago?" she replied.

"It was so long ago. Eighty years. Every year since we've come back to this, our old oak tree. He's one hundred and I'm plus two. A tree like this sees a lot through its long years in the woods. When a special soul comes along, it loves to spend some time with them. To have that person sit with it gives the tree more joy than even the summer sun can. To thank you, the tree shares a tale of its time. Sometimes a horrible event, most often as this, a special, happy time. We made this our tree when we gave our love to it. Now it will remember you too, never forget it."

Megan watched the old couple hug the oak tree. They held each other beneath boughs and shared a kiss. Then with a wave and smile, they disappeared the way they had come. Filled with magic, and enchanted with awe, Megan left the woods once more.

Remember to respect and love the trees you see in the woods. They remember what happens around them and hold it within them. Never will they forget those special times through the seasons of their long lives. If you make a beautiful memory in the woods, give some of that love to the tree. It will thank you, even if you carve into it. If you see a carving, study it, feel it and maybe the tree will share its story with you. For there's always a story behind the heart-shaped carving in the old oak tree.

***Judge's Comments:*** *What a delightful magical tale. One that makes one feel that the woods are indeed mysterious. Mother nature at her best. I felt this story could be lengthened, perhaps into a novel, including events of the era, stories of the war, etc. Well done.*

# HOT DATE
## By MAUREEN EDWARDS
### Genre – Chick Lit

Zoe pulled down on the flimsy, faded Yankee baseball cap covering her long black hair, hoping to hide her stench. She had been held in the cold room for hours, staring at the two-sided mirror. Biting her lip, she jumped when she saw the blue-suited brute who had arrested her. He slammed the door with a scowl and carefully placed a black four-inch Gucci shoe on the table, pushing it toward her. She grabbed it, slipping it on her bare dirty, cold foot.

He placed a pad and pen on the table. "Can we go through tonight's events *this time* in a calmer manner? No shouting. No calling me 'Tarzan of the Jungle.' I'm Detective Rick Anderson. What'd you say?"

Zoe rolled her eyes. "I've been calm since you dragged me outta' the restaurant in handcuffs! You didn't have to swing me over your shoulder!"

He rustled his dark brown hair, as he plopped into the chair opposite her. "You nearly broke your fancy shoe in the commotion, Ms. Samuels."

Zoe folded her hands. "It's either Zoe or, Dr. Samuels."

Rick cleared his throat, distracted for a second by her flawless skin. "Doctor of what?"

Sitting taller, chest out, Zoe said, "Psychiatry. I work with female prisoners in jail." Gulping, she hoped that little tidbit might score points with the breathtaking George Clooney clone.

Squinting, he stared closer. "Do you have different color eyes?" He leaned forward with a quizzical brow. "One is brown, and one is green if I'm not mistaken?"

A blush rushed to her cheeks. "My eyes are green." She spoke in a whisper. "I have colored contacts, and one popped out with the situation!"

Rick sat back. "Zoe, you're not arrested but your boyfriend..."

She banged her perfectly manicured hands on the table. "He is not my *boyfriend*. It was a blind date, run amuck! My client - "

Rick softly interjected, "From the women's prison?"

Zoe leaned her head to the side. "I proved she was innocent, and she wanted to do something nice for me."

Rick's eyebrows were raised. "So, she set you up with a felon?"

Zoe gulped hard. "She was *trying* to be nice. He chose a five-star restaurant, for God's sake! The chef is known for his fried shrimp which, by the way, was *amazing*. I mean, he excused himself from the table a few times, but I didn't know what he was doing!"

He threw the pen down. "You didn't know?"

She pushed up the sleeves to her POLICE oversized sweatshirt. "Not a clue! He ordered a souffle as it was my birthday last week. I thought it was sweet of him, and as I leaned over to kiss him *on the cheek.*"

He pointed to her head. "Is that when it happened?"

She ripped off the Yankee cap revealing her burnt, uneven hair. "Yes."

Rick covered his mouth. "Go on."

19

Zoe squirmed in her seat. She grabbed her singed hair and held it. "The candles set my hair on fire."

He jumped up. "Did he plan it?"

She jumped up too. "Are you kidding me? Do you think I wanted my hair to get set on fire and for six waiters to throw water pitchers over me?"

Rick turned his back to her, attempting to contain a giggle.

Zoe pleaded. "I swear *to God* I had no idea what he was doing."

Rick pushed the notepad and pen to her. "I believe you. He admitted you had nothing to do with him stealing customers' wallets and cellphones. I also spoke with your client, and she corroborated your story, so you'll be able to go once you write it down."

Zoe grabbed the pen and wrote as fast as she could. Rick couldn't believe she even needed a blind date, to begin with! He admired her faith in humanity, and boy, was she stunning.

Gently Zoe pushed the pen and notepad towards him, then stifled a yawn.

Rick gave her a bottle of water, and her cellphone, saying, "You've had a long night. How about I take you home?" She nodded, wiping away a tear.

In silence, Rick led Zoe, walking a few steps behind him, out to his SUV. He held the passenger side door open. "We're taking my car since I'm off duty now."

Zoe hopped in, sighing, "I do appreciate this."

As Rick turned the car on, Britney Spears 'Toxic' began playing in high decibels. He laughed out loud, "Sorry, one of my guilty pleasures."

Zoe's feet started to tap. "I hear you! I saw her in Vegas! She's awesome!"

Pulling up at Zoe's apartment complex, Rick was disappointed it was not further away. "Sorry I was tough on you. Just doing my job."

Pressing the buttons on her cell phone but with no luck, Zoe said, "I get it. Jeeze, my phone is dead. I guess my wallet is the evidence?"

Stopping at the entrance of her building, he saw the doorman watching them. "Yes, but I'll work on it for you."

Zoe fumbled with her keys. "That's nice of you." She rested her hand on his bare arm and noticed how soft his skin was. "Sorry if I was a snip. It was a long, embarrassing night."

"You handled it well," Rick stammered.

"Hey, you're starting to sound rather sweet, Rick," Zoe said as she climbed out of the car. "It's a nice side of you to see. Night." As she snuck into her apartment, butterflies swarmed in her tummy; still, she hoped no one would see her.

Once she entered her apartment, Zoe plugged her phone into the charger. She wanted to google Rick as soon as she could to get some information on him. But first, she needed a shower.

Coming out of the shower, she was drying off, when she heard her phone buzz with a text message from an unknown number. Opening the text she found a photo of Rick with Britney Spears. She laughed out loud for the first time in hours.

Suddenly her heart leaped out of her chest as she read his message: *Dinner soon? And you owe me a Yankee hat.*

*Judges' Comments:* *A short sweet story about new beginnings. Something to make one smile. But also a warning to be careful who you go on a blind date with, ha ha.*

# THE DARKNESS OF DANIEL
## By LAWRENCE DRACUT
### Genre - Mystery

It has been several months since my friend Daniel has passed away. Finally, I have finished dealing with the financial aspect of his estate, and now I am left with the unenviable task of making sense of the reams of notes he had accumulated during his lifetime.

I had always known him as an extremely sociable, positive although somewhat complex individual for most of his life, so was surprised and disturbed by what I was now reading.

His poems, dozens of unfinished stories, and several satirical Christmas songs, everything he had ever created but never shared with the world. They have left me with a sense of sadness and even guilt that is difficult to explain. I am distraught at the dark and depressing thoughts that I only now realise must have tormented him these past twenty-odd years.

Throughout many of his papers, he expressed a feeling of not being able to fit in at any level of society; or indeed in the culture of several of the countries, he had lived in. 'Where do I belong,' was written dozens of times in the margins of his papers. I could almost feel his anguish rising off the paper. Reading this, I recall asking him a few years ago, that in all of the photographs I had seen of him, why he never smiled. His answer had been a simple, 'because I have forgotten how to.'

It appears as though he spent many of the early morning hours trying to justify why he should even continue living. I know that he had a few friends like me, but sometimes I noticed the loneliness was seeping through the cracks of his public facade. He needed someone to watch his favourite movies with when he could share the funny parts he loved or those that moved you to tears. Only now do I understand how lonely and unhappy he was. He needed someone to share his life with.

I knew he would frantically write what his mind had created, often into the middle of the night; but I also knew how intensely he disliked the actual process of writing. Once he had produced a story in its entirety in his mind; the endless correcting and rewriting he only saw as a waste of time. I do not know if it was laziness on his part or the pure frustration of having to put on paper what his mind had written out perfectly from beginning to end.

Either way, it was his dislike of this process that had led him to invent a computer program that he believed would relieve him of this tedium. It would however also lead to his eventual demise.

I know from our many conversations that Daniel had always been interested in practically all religions and ideologies. His thoughts, and opinions ranged from an unquestionable belief in an omnipotent God to theories on this same divine one being a visitor from an alien planet.

No matter which particular opinion I occasionally agreed with, he would then inevitably argue the opposing opinion convincingly. I often wondered if perhaps I was sometimes a source of entertainment for him. He was also prone to throwing into the mix, that in his opinion, organised religion was the source of most of this world's evil. Never did I leave his company without some small doubt creeping into my own beliefs.

There were many occasions when Daniel, I, and a few selected acquaintances dabbled in the darker arts of the Ouija board. Often there were many interesting, and sometimes frightening, unexplainable results in our futile attempts to determine if there was indeed an after-life.

We all had the same questions. 'Are we reincarnated? Does life exist after death? Do we have a purpose?' For those of us that participated in these sessions, it was fascinating, but for Daniel, it became an obsession.

Being an avid reader of all types of research on new uses for drugs, legal or otherwise, coupled with an interest in medical technology advances, he was steered towards what he theorized was the answer to his main objective. He believed that it was possible to transfer his thoughts, and therefore his stories, directly to his computer printer. This would leave him free to create, without the tediousness of having to type.

His most recent scribbled, and almost indecipherable notes, showed me that he had somehow obtained a variety of hallucinogenic drugs and opioids. Also, some electrical sensors that he would use to connect his brain directly to his computer.

To complicate me further, I must confess to never having had the need, or desire to study the anatomy of neurology, so must admit that I was somewhat at a loss when attempting to understand the information I was looking at. He wrote, that the 100 billion neurons in the brain, that transmit messages to the specific lobes of the brain, both chemical and electrical signals, are used through the use of neurotransmitters. Any deviance in this process would affect the desired outcome. His studies included how these changes affected   the personality of people with untreated and treated schizophrenia, and other mental health issues. He concluded that it was all due to this interruption of the neurotransmitter process.

Critically, what Daniel had focussed on was that artificial neural networks have been created by many scientists, and it was their studies that he had concentrated his work on. His theory was simple and to my mind even logical. With the correct hallucinogenic chemicals and other drugs, his brain would be able to convert his thoughts into electronic impulses and thus direct them to his computer printer.

There followed months of what I now read were horrific experiments on himself, until eventually, he had achieved his goal. Although this was not without some unforeseen consequences.

In my last few visits with him, I noticed that there were certain changes within his personality. He was becoming morose, often melancholy, saying how he had wasted many of the talents that he had been born with. Like many others before him, myself included, there was nothing to leave behind when he died.

Nothing to show that he had accomplished anything of consequence. He could think of nothing worse than being simply forgotten.

I failed to connect these changing moods with his recent recurring obsession with the age-old question of was there life, of any kind, after death. Unknown to me, he had decided, that there was one earth-shattering achievement he could fulfil, that would leave his mark on the history books. Something he would always be remembered for.

He had decided to use his creation to discover with irrefutable proof that there was life after death. But, to do so it would mean that he would have to die.

It must have been during one of his darkest and anguished nights when he was just tired of life. Also possibly fuelled by too many glasses of gin and tonic, that he decided it was time to put his theory to the test. Wearing a crudely made cap to hold the sensors in place, he next consumed carefully measured amounts of chodonystatin, orpthozaledine, codoflaxcine, and two hallucinogenics, the names of which were illegible. He had calculated that this combination would shut his body down quickly, yet give his brain several minutes of activity in which he would experience, and record what happens after you die.

The printer would record not only his dying thoughts but would transmit what he saw of his existence after his physical death.

I thank God that I was not the person who found him the next day; this, unfortunately, fell to the fate of his cleaning lady. In her statement to the police she said, that she had found him leaning backward in his office chair; more upsetting than finding him dead was the look on his face. The way she described it, it was as if his soul was being tortured. That his last few breaths had been tormented by whatever he was experiencing.

There was now only one final task that I had to perform to conclude my promised duties. I had to examine the last few pages that had been printed out.

'Well, my friends, I have just taken the final step in this miserable existence, there is no going back. I believe that I am now officially deceased as I am unable to feel any parts of my body moving. Any moment now I am expecting my brain to shut down. I do not know whether this will happen instantly or slowly, but we shall soon know.'

The next page contained a series of jumbled letters and words which I find pointless in trying to decipher, but it continues with his last transmission, for want of a better description.

'I can no longer see anything that is in this room but, I feel a sense of peace, so think that I am now leaving this world, my soul preparing to enter another dimension. There is a light that appears to be coming from a cone-shaped tunnel, although it seems far away it appears quite bright. Too bright, almost blinding as I can see nothing else but that. I believe that I should now have some beautiful awareness of my soul leaving my body and entering the tunnel. My late family or ancestors will be greeting me soon, or even an angel guide.'

There was a foreboding, seemingly endless pause at this point, then he continued. 'Something is happening, the light is dimming. It's gone, the tunnel has disappeared too. It's not supposed to be like this. It's getting darker, too dark. I don't like this, I expected something wonderful, not this. I don't like this at all. I am frightened now.'

'I seem to be losing control of my thoughts.'

'There is no one here for me, no one at all. Oh dear God, I was wrong. It's just black now, nothing but pitch black, I cannot see, there is nothing, nothing, nothing, noth......................'

As in his life, fate had dealt him one more cruel blow, as at this point there had been an electric power failure. Only for a few minutes but enough to shut down his computer and printer.

Was there more? Did he find that there was an afterlife? Or was the blackness how it ended?

"Did you find the answerers you were looking for, Daniel?" I said aloud to his empty room, "Or did you just cease to exist?"

I sat on his sofa for one last time, wondering if I should share his story with the world.

I decided yes.

Although the proof of an afterlife would have sealed his place in history, his name will still be known. But, it will be known as the man who tried to answer the ultimate question and, although he failed, he gave his life in attempting to do so.

Leaving his home for the last time, I closed the door and quietly, said, "Goodbye, Daniel; wherever you are."

*Judge's Comments: What a spooky story that shows the fine line between genius and madness. A well-written piece. Well done.*

# THE RELUCTANT SINGER

## By JOY LYNN

### Genre – Contemporary Fiction

**Dedicated to my wonderful husband Graeme. Sadly no longer here but who was always my rock.**

Beth had been Mrs Elizabeth Warren for so long, that when Richard died, she did not know how to become just Beth again. His passing had been unexpected. A massive shock. And for the first few months, she had felt completely bewildered and lost.

Sometimes she had even felt angry, thinking, 'how could you leave me on my own? What am I supposed to do now?'

Well, now she had her answer!

She gazed up at the cruise ship, wondering how on earth she had got here. Susie and Janice were her best friends, but they had landed her with this. As she stood on the dock, she could hear their voices in her head.

"You need to move on, Beth. You're still young, with years of life and adventures ahead of you. Just get out there and do something new."

In fairness, as the months passed, she had adjusted to her new life as a widow and her friends had been super-supportive. Then out of a clear blue sky, Susie and Janice had come back from a cruise with their husbands, going on and on about it. So, without really thinking about it, Beth had gone into the local travel agents and booked the next available cruise on the Seascape.

Here she was! Standing at the bottom of the gangplank waiting to embark with her luggage already on board the ship. On the dock, people all around her were chattering excitedly and suddenly she felt very lonely and unsure of herself. This was when she would have expected Richard to take charge.

'Now, is not a good time to have second thoughts,' she silently chided herself, 'it's too late to change your mind.'

Taking a deep breath, she stepped forward and was soon greeted by a lovely smiling young man who offered to show her to her cabin. 'This will be my bolthole if it all gets too much for me,' Beth thought.

'That is if I can ever find my way back here again!'

There was a sheet of paper on the bed called 'Cruise News' and when Beth looked at it, she was amazed to find it detailed tons of information that she would need for the next day. There were dozens of activities listed from early morning to late evening.

"Goodness me," Beth chuckled to herself. "If I start each day with a mile walk around the deck at 7.00 am, join all these activities and then finish off in the disco at 1.00 am I will be utterly exhausted by the end of the holiday!"

Suddenly one particular entry leapt off the page at her. The Seascape Choir will meet in the Starlight Lounge at 2.00 pm. No experience is necessary but, if you enjoy singing, we would love to see you.

'I would love to do that,' Beth thought. She had been in the school choir and had thought of joining something at university, but when she met Richard at the end of the first term, they had immediately become inseparable.

Richard had simply not been musical but was completely and utterly tone-deaf. He hadn't been negative about her singing, but he wasn't positive either.

So, that had been the end of her singing career.

However, every once in a while, whenever she heard a particular piece of music, Beth would remember the joy that singing had brought her. And then she wondered what it would be like to be in a choir again.

Well, here was her chance!

Waking up the next morning, Beth felt excited for her first full day of the cruise. After breakfast, she went to a meeting on the daily schedule called 'Singles Ahoy,' which was to encourage all single travellers to get together. It had sounded awful but from somewhere she found a little bit of courage, noticing that when she arrived everyone else had looked as apprehensive as her.

Beth smiled tentatively at a man who was sitting on his own and, on a whim, she sat down next to him. Nobody was more surprised at this than she was. He looked nothing like Richard – thinking about it later, she realised that it was his warm and friendly smile that had drawn her to him.

"Hi," she said. "I'm Beth. I've never been on a cruise before and don't know what to expect. It's also my first holiday on my own for years, so I'm feeling a bit nervous."

The man looked relieved. "Me too. It's all seems a bit overwhelming, doesn't it? I wasn't sure whether to come or not. I'm Larry by the way."

"Lovely to meet you, Larry."

An hour later, Beth and Larry were sitting in the Bosun's Bar having a latte and still chatting.

"What are you doing after lunch?" Larry asked her.

Beth pointed excitedly at the Cruise News. "I am going to this choir rehearsal. I can hardly wait. But it's been so long since I tried singing, I think my voice might be a little rusty!"

"Oh!" said Larry cheerfully. "I can't hold a tune in a bucket. I love music, but if I ever sang, it would make the dogs howl and peel the enamel off your teeth."

Beth was disappointed as she had been hoping to

persuade Larry to go with her to the rehearsal, however, they arranged to meet up afterwards so she could tell him all about it.

Just before 2.00 pm, Beth was sitting in the Starlight Lounge and, with a sense of anticipation, she looked around at the other people present. Some were obviously couples, but most people seemed to be on their own.

Shortly afterwards, a member of staff walked in and sat at the piano.

"Hello. I'm Phil, the musical director for our onboard band. Now, if you know what voice part you are, can you please move to sit in your sections, soprano, alto, tenor and bass. Ladies, if you are not sure can you please sit with the sopranos."

Beth knew she was an alto, so moved to sit where Phil had indicated. Looking around she thought there was a good balance of voices. Still, she was feeling slightly disappointed – to her surprise – that Larry had not come to the rehearsal, despite what he had said.

"Excellent," said Phil. "Now, on the table at the front are some sheets for you to collect. If you read music, pick up one of the scores but, don't worry if you don't, just take one of the lyric sheets."

Although she was apprehensive when she collected her sheet music, Beth felt pleased that she had learned music at school. Mind you this was probably not something Richard would have understood.

Phil started the rehearsal and she felt as if the next hour flew by. Inside her head, she thought that her voice sounded good, although she knew that she had never sung for Richard. She could hardly wait to tell Larry all about it.

Over the next few days, the music was to come at them fast and furious. It would include songs from Les Misérables and The Sound of Music, music she was well aware her late husband had not enjoyed. She even recognised that Phil was not easy to work with, and some people who did not read music were clearly struggling a little. On occasions, he could be something of a prima donna.

However, to her intense pleasure, Beth realised she was relishing the process, although she was worried that some of the other choir members would just give up. After all, they were on holiday and were there to enjoy themselves, not to be told off for not getting it right.

"He needs to realise that not everyone is a musical genius," Beth told Larry after one particularly difficult rehearsal.

Still, despite Phil's attitude, and because she was remembering her love of singing, every time Beth came out of the rehearsal, she felt energised and uplifted. It was as if she was always beaming with pleasure when she joined Larry afterwards for a latte in their favourite bar.

At the fourth rehearsal, Phil had a big surprise for them. He told them that they would be putting on a concert in the theatre on the last day of the cruise. A murmur of excitement ran around the choir. Singing in front of a live audience would make them work even harder, making sure the music was word and note perfect.

Then came an even bigger surprise.

"I would like some solos and duets to fit into the programme alongside the choral numbers," Phil said.

"So, if any of you would like to volunteer then please stay behind at the end of the rehearsal to have a chat with me. There is only one condition – that you know the song well enough to perform it without music. I won't have any time to practice with you other than after choir rehearsals."

For the rest of the rehearsal, Beth could not stop thinking about it. Richard had never encouraged her to pursue her love of music. In fact, she could not remember him encouraging her with much else either, although he had always been loving and protective towards her. She had never sung a solo before and was not sure whether she was brave enough to even try. On impulse, she texted Larry whose response was simply 'go 4 it.'

Beth was still not sure, so was surprised when she found herself at the end of the rehearsal standing next to Phil at the piano saying, "If you have no one else then I'll give it a try."

"Excellent," he said. "What would you like to sing?"

Beth thought quickly. Suddenly, one of her favourite songs from when she was in the school choir popped into her head. She knew the words off by heart and had always enjoyed singing it. But that was over 40 years ago. Could she still remember it?

"'I don't know how to love him,' from Jesus Christ Superstar," she quickly said before she changed her mind.

"Good choice," said Phil and he started to play the introduction. Beth's voice was wobbly to start with but, as she started on the second verse, she felt herself becoming more confident. By the end of the piece, she was singing out loud and clear.

"That was quite good," Phil said, "but just take a breath before the last note so that you can hold it on a bit longer. Other than that, not a bad first attempt. Now, just sing it one more time for me."

Working with Phil, she realised, was enjoyable. In no way was he being difficult and, as a coach, he certainly had some redeeming qualities. She realised he just wanted the choir to be as good as it could be. Strangely, Beth did too. As Beth left the lounge there was a spring in her step and she was feeling incredibly pleased with herself.

Over the next few days, the song became like an ear-worm – she ran over the words in her head whilst trying to get to sleep, she hummed it to herself whilst lying on the sunbed, she sang it to herself in the shower.

By the day of the concert she knew she was ready.

Beth was nervous and a bit distracted when she sat down for lunch with Larry so when he said he would scribble his contact details on the menu she barely gave it a thought. She pushed it into her handbag without realising what she was doing.

As the choir walked onto the theatre stage Beth looked out at the audience, realising there were certainly two or three hundred people in attendance. She could see Larry sitting on the left-hand side about 10 rows back waving at her and giving her an energetic 'thumbs up.'

Standing in her place Beth felt full of anticipation and nervous energy. As soon as Phil started playing the opening bars of the first number, something clicked, and she lost herself in the feeling of the music.

The choral pieces were going very well, with the audience being enthusiastic about the solo - 'Summertime' - which was sung by one of the sopranos. Beth was extremely impressed and started to worry that her solo would be a bit of a let-down.

Next came a duet - 'Something Stupid' - sung by a husband and wife who obviously had performed it many times as their party piece. Beth was not sure that the audience loved it quite as much as the singers did. It did, however, leave her feeling certain that she had something that the audience would enjoy.

When it was time for her solo, she walked up to the microphone and looked out at the audience. Her knees felt wobbly, her throat was dry and there were butterflies in her stomach. Then she caught Larry's eye, just for a moment and knew that she was ready.

Phil started playing, Beth took a deep breath, and her voice rang out clearly across the auditorium. She put her heart and soul into it, singing for pure joy. It was the most wonderful feeling. She did not want it to end so she held the last note for as long as she could. For a heartbeat there was silence and then she heard the applause, and someone – probably Larry – cheering.

Beth gave a small bow before moving back to stand in her place for the final choral number. She could see other choir members smiling at her and mouthing "well done." She felt a rush of pride that she had put aside her nerves and sung so well.

More to the point, people had enjoyed it.

After the concert, Larry rushed up to her and gave her a quick hug. "You were wonderful," he said, "I didn't know you could sing like that."

"Neither did I," Beth said smiling. "I could do it all over again!"

"Let's go and have a celebratory latte instead," said Larry, laughing.

Later that night, as Beth was getting ready in her cabin for her final night on board, she thought back over the past two weeks. She remembered how apprehensive she had been standing on the dock looking up at the ship. Now she felt thrilled at having enjoyed her holiday much more than she thought she would. As she was packing, she caught sight of the menu with Larry's contact details on. She dropped it into her suitcase. A telephone call wouldn't hurt, would it?

The music had changed everything.

No longer was she just Mrs. Elizabeth Warren, widow - she was now Beth, single, independent woman, ready for her next adventure. For the first time in a long while, she felt confident and comfortable in her skin. Whether it was teaching, coaching, or just singing her heart out in a local choir, she knew that music would now be the heart and soul of her life.

She closed the cabin door and walked down the corridor towards the lift. As she passed a couple coming the other way, she heard them say, "That's the singer!"

'Yes, I am,' thought Beth smiling to herself. 'Yes, I am!'

*Judge's Comments: And that's the way to do it, as we say when you feel you need a change in life. This is a story of 'He (or I should say) She who dares Wins. It shows the power that the human race has when it needs to overcome and quell those silly fears. Lovely tale. Well written.*

# BOYS AT THE BEACH
## By MAUREEN EDWARDS
### Genre – Contemporary Fiction

Grandma appeared in her grandson's room. "Morning, Pat! What would you like to do today?"

Pat had a slight lisp due to a recent front tooth falling out. "Grandma, *you* know! I want to play with Eric!"

Grandma swallowed hard as she pulled out Pat's favorite blue shorts and a white T-shirt with an orange tiger standing on his hind legs. This outfit always made Pat happy.

Pat was able to put his clothes on fast these days. Seeing the tiger he roared, "I bet today we can go in the water! It's gonna be a hot one!"

"Maybe." Grandma bit her lip. "How about I put my suit on too? The waves might be a little rough! I know you are turning four next week, and you're big and strong, but I would love to jump in the water with you; if it's OK with you and Eric, of course!"

"I'll ask him. He's always happy to do stuff with you, Grandma."

Pat put his socks on one by one, just as Grandma had shown him the week before. Next, he put his sneakers on, snapping the Velcro across. He always chose those sneakers instead of the ones with the laces. Too much trouble and time. It took away from the fun! He stood up tall, pushed his uneven blonde bangs off his face, and cheered, "Ready to roll!"

Grandma couldn't help but laugh. "Ha! Where'd you hear that saying from?"

"Eric! He told me he heard it on the news."

Pat ran out of the bedroom, leaving Grandma to tidy up a bit; placing his dirty underwear and damp pajamas into the washing bin. Yet again they reeked of urine. Grandma always fixated on Pat's plaid bedspread. His brown dresser. His half-full closet. She straightened the 'P' on his wall as it was a little crooked. Her brows furrowed when she had to adjust the 'A' and 'T' to straighten them out too. She hummed, 'The Wheels on the Bus,' as she touched each letter with tender care, stepping back to make sure it looked perfect over Pat's bed, which sat on the left side of the room. She stood frozen for a moment and stared at his name, picking off the skin from around her thumbnail until it nearly bled.

Pat bellowed, "Grandma, let's go!"

Grandma caught her breath and shuffled out not looking back, slamming the door behind her. "We're off for the day! One minute, Pat. I know you are excited but let me get all the stuff together."

She had packed the lunches already. Due to food allergies, she had to be extra careful. Never, ever nuts again! She could not bear another accident. Grilled cheese on gluten-free bread, dry, no mayo. Snacks were always green apple slices that stayed fresh all day since Grandma placed the frozen juice boxes around them like a caring hug. Pat was so fast, so determined to run that sometimes she forgot to pack the food, which became a huge issue. She was well used to the routine now, trying to make every day as perfect as possible. According to her daughter, who shot the orders all the time from afar, it was imperative to keep Pat structured.

Grandma found Pat swaying back and forth impatiently by the door. "About time, Grandma! Shake a leg!"

She chugged a big gulp of water. "Hey, I am not as young as I used to be, kiddo."

Then she piled the lunches into the oversized bright orange beach bag. The weatherman was right! It feels as if they would have a hot one today.

"What temperature does the number say on the thermometer?" Ever the retired pre-school teacher, Grandma conducted circle time activities with Pat, when he least expected it.

His brown eyes squinted, and he said, "Sixty-seven. I kinda forget how...."

She threw her bathing suit into the bag. "Sixty-nine...."

He was clapping and jumping up and down. "Seventy! That's right. I was close this time." As he pointed and counted to the numbers above the line on the thermometer with a whisper.

Grandma whistled. "Terrific, kiddo. You know your numbers, up to my age now! Smarter than anyone I *ever* taught in school. Come on. We're off!"

Pat, ready to leave, turned the doorknob with his

left hand and pushed the sizeable glass-paned door with his right hand. It had been so heavy for him in the past but not any longer. The door opened so fast he almost lost his balance.

Grandma's eyebrows lowered. "You're getting stronger every day opening that door. Thanks for being such a gentleman!"

"I learned that from Eric. He always says to be polite to you."

Grandma stopped on the porch placing the beach bag down. She did not have her keys handy and felt around in her pockets until she touched the cold, hard metal edges. Usually, she had them in her hands. This was not part of the daily routine for Pat, and she felt him staring, until she said, "Here we are! The key! I almost misplaced it. So silly of me." Locking the front door, she pulled the handle a few times to make sure it was shut securely. "Honey, do you want to make sure Grandma has locked up?"

Using both his hands he twisted the doorknob two or three times, but it didn't move. "You're such a good helper, making sure we are safe, and that nothing happens to the house when we are at the beach. Let's roll, kiddo," and Grandma cheered.

He high-fived her. "I'm getting to be like the man around the house, right Grandma?"

Grabbing him, she hugged him hard for several seconds. It always seemed to help him refocus. "OK, kiddo. The beach, the seagulls, the water, and Eric are all waiting for us!"

"Yay!" Pat ran as fast as his little legs could carry him to the top of the dune. She always let him lead the way. Her daughter insisted that would build his confidence. But, he also followed Grandma's rule to stop and wait for her. He was her little angel.

Following behind, Grandma was fully aware that their house was the only one within half a mile of the nearest neighbor. The need to lock the door was not high on her list of things to do every day, but that had changed since starting to take care of Pat full time. It was apparent, with his nightmares a while ago, that he needed to feel safe in every way possible. She had forgotten to lock the door one time, and that had been a disaster.

Grandma was huffing and puffing more and more as the days went by. Exhausted from Pat's constant need for care, something would have to give, sooner or later, except she had no idea how to broach the subject with her daughter. When would the right time be? A few more days? Another month? She would have to play it by ear as it was only a few months since things had changed. She never counted the days to summer vacation or winter break, as she had while being a teacher for over thirty years. But this was a lot for her, no matter what the circumstances. Blinking quickly and perspiring everywhere, Grandma stopped for a moment, looking at Pat's face light up as he stared at the beach. She could almost see his wheels turning as he rubbed his hands together, looking for Eric ready to have another fantastic day in paradise!

Grandma joined him huffing, attempting to catch her breath. "My Pat, you are such a good listener. I don't ever thank you enough for following my directions and waiting for me." She plopped the bag down, grabbing some more water for a sip. "It takes my old lady's bones a while to get here, and you seem to be getting faster and faster!" She threw the bottle back in the bag then put her hands on her hips. "My, what a day!"

Pat took Grandma's hand placing it on his head. She began to rub it gently. This was something new that he liked. It seemed to help him calm down for a moment.

Pat whispered, "Can I run, Grandma? Can I run and play with Eric, please? He's already started the sandcastle!" His face lit up, anticipating her response.

Grandma kissed the top of his head. "Go, honey, and tell him I said hello! I'll watch you guys from here today. I'm a little tired. I'll keep lunch up here, too."

Just as he was about to grab the beach bag, he stopped for a second, looked at Grandma, and said, "Thanks for being my friend, Grandma," and with that, he sped off.

Grandma choked back a tear as she watched him. His feet were kicking up the sand as he dragged the bag of beach toys that was almost as tall as him. Grandma had shown him where he could play on the sand, far from the breaking waves. He was always such a good listener. Dumping a load of toys out onto the sand, she heard him explaining to Eric how they would build the sandcastle today. Same thing, day in and day out.

"You can do this too!" Pat lifted the pail slowly to build the tower higher and higher, almost waist high now. This took nearly the entire day, as it did every day! To Pat, the sand felt like gooky mud, but he knew he had Eric by his side to help lift the wet, moist, cold sand into the blue plastic bucket. His feet were buried in a slight hole as the low tide trickled back and forth, whispering goodbye to those who visited.

As the sun began to set, Grandma sat on her towel just a few feet away from Pat and Eric, glancing at her trashy novel while she eavesdropped on Pat's conversation. She heard, "Good job," "Keep it up," "You got this" constantly. 'Pat was always so positive with his friend,' she thought.

Suddenly her phone buzzed, and she saw it was her daughter. The calls came too few and far between for her liking. Sighing heavily, she answered with a fake happy tone. "Hi, honey! Will you be coming home soon?" She listened to her daughter's excuse after excuse for staying away. "Oh, Pat is getting so big, honey. It's wonderful. He is sweet and kind. He reminds me of you!" Grandma bit her fingernail as her daughter rambled on about work, money, and her estranged husband. "I understand."

She glanced at the time and stood up, looking to see if the sandcastle was nearly done for the day. "Yes, he's with Eric now. They are safe and sound, honey." Nodding she said, "Do you want me to tell Pat anything special today?" She bit her lip. "OK, dear.

Call again. Please." Her lips were forming a few other words, but her daughter had hung up, as she said in midair, "We love you, too."

Realizing it was almost dinner time Grandma said it was time to go. Pat took his pail and screamed, "Fine. Go home. Who wants you here anyway, Eric?"

It was so loud and clear Grandma jumped up and ran to Pat. This was not like him. He and Eric never fought! Ever! She called out, "Pat! Pat! I'm coming, honey!" Her heart was racing. Her eyes were like daggers. Nothing and no one was going to upset her sweet Pat. No one. Nothing ever again!

Pat was sobbing, gripping the pail and shovel tightly. He was inconsolable. As he opened his eyes to see her approach, he threw the treasured toys into the sand. He grabbed onto her waist and sobbed for what seemed to be hours, yet it was just a few seconds. She rubbed his back as he cried.

Finally, he began to take deep, calming breaths. Letting go of her slowly, he wiped his face. "Can we go home, please, Grandma? I want to do something else today. I don't want to play with Eric anymore. And I told him not to eat the nuts at lunch! I told him!"

Grandma took his flushed face into her hands. "I know you did, honey. He's gone. Whatever you want, honey." Hand in hand, they walked in silence back to the house. Pat sniffled most of the way, while Grandma wracked her brain, trying to think about what to do when they got into the house, deciding it best to follow Pat's lead. Sitting at the kitchen table he put his head down on his arms.

"Grandma, can I have something to drink?"

She handed him the juice box from his lunch bag since he hadn't drunk it at lunchtime whilst on the beach. He sipped the juice without talking or making eye contact with her. Sitting with him, she drank a little juice herself. Her stomach was doing somersaults as she heard the slurping sound of the empty juice box, unsure what Pat would do, or say next. She watched him out of the corner of her eye, then tilted her head. "So, what do you want to do now, honey? Do you want to talk about anything?"

Pat shook his head. "Grandma, I know I'm a big boy, but I really am tired. Could I take a nap with you today in your room?"

She rubbed his hand. "That sounds like the perfect way to end the day. How about we get a toy from your room to keep you company while we rest?"

Pat nodded and walked to his room in silence with his shoulders hunched over. She followed a step behind. Running his hand over all the stuffed animals on his bed, Pat stood still. "I don't want any of these, Grandma."

Grandma stood in the hallway, careful not to intrude in his space. "Pat honey, whatever you like. Take whatever you like."

Pat walked over to the other bed and looked at the pile of bears, finally taking the white bear with the red heart. He hugged it and walked out of his bedroom.

Grandma gulped. "He will make a nice friend for naptime. I'll be right in," and she kissed the top of Pat's head before he walked towards her bedroom.

Standing in Pat's bedroom was choking Grandma. She noticed how stale the air was, and how it smelled of musty wood. Her eyes rolled up to the ceiling. She always tried hard to avoid one side of the room. Walking over to the other twin bed with a plaid bedspread she glanced at the crooked letters. Tears fell down her face. Touching each letter she straightened them out, starting with the 'E' then the 'R' followed by the 'I' and finally the 'C.'

*Judge's Comments: This story shows the modern world we live in and the pressures we place on others. It is quite a spooky tale with an unusual ending, not one I was expecting to read. Well done.*

# SPLASH, SPLASH

## By COLIN DEVONSHIRE

## Genre - Horror

"Thank you, darling. How wonderful, a break together, I never thought we'd do it," Mags said.

"Anything for the prettiest wife in the world," Robin smiled.

"Don't get carried away with your praise, especially when you don't mean it." She chuckled.

"We've had a nightmare year or two. A break will be good for us all. How do you feel?"

"So far, so good. It was tough getting out of the house that first day. But now, six months on, I not only escaped my self-built prison, but I also made steady progress. I left the village. Now here I am, with my family, on holiday."

"I'm proud of you, and so are the children. Where are they?" asked Robin.

They are too young to understand, but thanks for saying it. They ran to the beach without unpacking their stuff," said a joyful mother.

"Are they okay on their own?"

"Just look out of the window. There they are, running across the sand. Not a care in the world."

"Shall we leave them to it? We could catch up with another thing that's been missing from our lives." And he grinned as he wrapped his arms around his wife. The cheeky young woman he had met all those years ago at university was back. She tugged him towards the bedroom.

"Just a sec," she mouthed as he unclipped her bra.

"Okay, where were we," she said, returning from sneaking a look outside.

"You don't have to check them every minute, you know," said Robin, lifting the quilt and patting the bed.

The children had worn themselves out leaping the waves. Now it was time to search for the enemy - crabs.

"Lizzie, look, a monster," said Jay.

"Not as big as mine," said Lizzie as she freed a gluey blob from a discarded Coke bottle.

"That is not a crab. You are cheating. What is it? Is it alive?"

"I don't know. Ouch! It bit me," said Lizzie, shaking blobs of blood from her thumb.

"Over there, there's another one," said Jay, pointing at a sandy puddle. He moved towards it, then yelped.

"Look out behind you," said Lizzie too slowly. "There's another one of those things."

"Jesus, that hurt. Come on, we'd better go home," said big brother Jay.

The children sprinted up the beach, clambered over some rocks, and burst through the back gate and into the kitchen.

"Mum, Dad, something has hurt us," screamed Lizzie at the bottom of the stairs, "The arch-rivals got us."

Robin's concentration split in two, Mags' bliss was shattered.

"Oh God, what's happened? Get dressed quickly." Robin said as he nudged his wife, and they fell out of bed.

Grabbing a robe, Mags bounded down the stairs, her husband two steps behind.

"What happened?" she asked.

"It bit my thumb." Lizzie held the damaged appendage out for her mother to see.

Jay balanced on one leg and raising the other, said, "It got me on the ankle, look."

Robin looked at the wounds. "Nasty, how did you do that?"

"Same as Lizzie's thumb. Something in the sand bit us," said Jay. Lizzie nodded furiously in agreement.

"What do you think, Mum?" asked Robin.

"It looks like a leech bite?" Mags said.

"Err, that sounds horrible," said Lizzie.

"I thought you only got leeches in freshwater?" asked Jay.

"Normally, yes, but there are some in warmer oceans."

"And the Channel is warmer? You are joking?" said Robin sarcastically.

"That's what I don't understand. Maybe it was something else," said Mags.

"How come you know so much about it, Mum," asked Jay.

"As you know, I've spent a lot of time indoors, most of it reading," she answered.

"I wish I was clever like you," said Lizzie.

"Keep going to school, then you will be clever, too. Now, run upstairs, unpack your things, and change for dinner," ordered Robin.

Later having done as they were told, the children plodded downstairs.

"I can't smell cooking. What are we eating? Don't say it's salad?" asked Jay.

"No. We are going out. If that is okay with you two?" said Robin.

"What about Mum, can she come?" asked Lizzie.

"Mummy is better now. Come on, let's go find a restaurant," said Robin.

While the children pulled their parents towards fast-food outlets, Robin and Lizzie had more original ideas for their meal. "Here we are, 'Olde English Pub and Restaurant' that's the place we spotted in the guidebook, highly recommended."

"Yes, looks lovely, a meal in the pub's garden. What do you fancy?" asked Robin.

"Wow, we've never been in a pub before," said Lizzie.

"Do they have burgers?… Ouch, what was that?"

Jay furiously scratched his ankle under the table. "Mum, I'm bleeding again!"

"Do you need a plaster?" a young girl said as she handed them the menus.

Mags grabbed paper tissues from the table, mopping the blood.

"Robin, look at this?" Mags pointed at the wound. "Something is wriggling under the blood."

The barmaid gagged as she backed away, the menus floated to the grass.

"We had better get to a hospital," said Robin, trying to stop his son from looking.

Arriving at the hospital Jay, supported by his parents, limped to the A&E counter, his trainer now full of blood.

"Come through, please," a nurse showed the way.

"Okay, young man," smiled the doctor, "please lie on the table. Let me remove your shoe and sock. Mmm... What did he do?" he asked, turning to Robin.

"Both he and his sister got nipped by something in the sea earlier. We cleaned it and popped on a Band-Aid, then it started itching and blood oozed out. His sister is outside with his Mum, do you want to look at her thumb too?"

"Let me look at this first, then I'll check her."

The nurse pulled off the plaster and gasped. Open-eyed, she stared at the doctor.

He started gently pulling at a blood-soaked worm. A worm with a mouth opening and closing, sucking in air. The doctor tugged harder; the worm wrapped itself around the pincers.

"Hold this," ordered the doctor. The nurse stepped closer and held the metal. The doctor scrabbled for another tool.

"You had better wait outside," he told Robin.

The worried father, in two minds, finally went and talked to Mags.

Mags and Lizzie weren't in view, Robin guessed they must be in the ladies. He waited.

"Aargh, get it off me."

Robin dashed towards his daughter's voice.

Mags' hands clamped hard onto a wash-hand basin, her feet rooted to the spot. She knotted her eyes shut. She couldn't bear to look at her daughter's hand. Lizzie's arm was outstretched, she was juddering her wrist, flicking blood up to the mirror.

"Mum, get it off me!"

"Nurse, nurse, come quick," shouted Robin from the doorway.

"You take my daughter. I'll look after my wife," ordered Robin.

"Mags, it's okay, relax, breathe deep and long. Come on, release your grip, let go of the basin, let's sit down," he said.

"It's starting again, I can't move," she quaked.

"I must go home," she wailed.

"You're okay, we can't leave the children."

He prised her hands away from the ceramic basin and gently led the shaking woman to the waiting room. "Will you be all right? I must check on Jay and Lizzie."

He didn't wait for an answer; he just dashed out to find the doctor.

"It's all my fault," she mumbled to his fast disappearing shoulders.

* * * * *

"Here we are, Maxie, are you ready for your run?"

The elderly chemist unclipped a battered and scored leather lead. The over-weight black Labrador waddled onto the beach, attempting to run, remembering those days as a pup. Now he was barely quicker than a walking pace as he made his way to the sea's edge, aged paws splashing ahead of his loving owner.

"Good boy, you enjoy your dip," she called after him.

The chemist kept to the dry fluffy sand, her eyes never leaving her beloved dog. Suddenly, Maxie's front legs buckled, his nose dipped into the seawater and wrinkled sand, as his front legs collapsed completely.

"Oh, no, Maxie, what is wrong?" called his owner, as she ran crying to her pet.

Crouching down in the sand, she lifted her pet's head from the water, noticing small lumps under the fur. The slight bumps were moving towards his chest.

"What the?... Aargh."

She felt mosquito bites from inside her rubber ankle boots. Trying to free her foot from the footwear, she toppled sideways onto the wet sand. Within seconds, circles of blood appeared on her legs. No longer mosquito bites, the pain jabbed and pricked her like a nest of bee stings.

Young lovers cuddled each other as they enjoyed a stroll to the pub along the seafront.

"What is happening over there?" a girl pointed.

"It looks like the old lady and her dog that passed us. Come on, they need help," the boyfriend answered and they both sprinted down the beach.

Within moments they too became covered in small biting creatures.

"Help, help," he called as he pressed the panic button on his phone, before disappearing under a cloud of dark grey.

* * * * *

In the bay, a dinghy floated on the tide where it was moored.

"How did you enjoy your first sailing lesson?" asked a proud father.

"Oh, wow, great, that was fun. When can we go again?" asked his daughter.

"Sounds like the weather will be fine again tomorrow. How about in the morning?"

"Brill Dad, thanks. What's that?" and she pointed to a black cloud moving towards their boat under the gentle waves.

"It looks like an overweight blubber-filled walrus," he smiled before leaning over the edge to look closer, his daughter sat next to him.

Behind them, slug-like creatures were sliding up and over the opposite side of the boat.

* * * * *

Further out in the bay, a Finnmaster 8 bobbed. Its owners were on the seabed, hoping they could find the shoulder bag their friend had flung overboard earlier.

They passed hand signals. The index finger rolled to meet the thumb, 'Okay', followed by pointing up, which meant enough searching for today.

"Nightmare," said Bobby as he spat out saltwater.

"Poor Sal, devastated at losing her favourite bag, and all her stuff in it," nodded Petra.

"What the hell was she thinking? She hurled it at him."

"You heard the row she was having with her 'new' friend."

"Not friends now, are they?" laughed Bobby.

"No, especially when she swung her bag at him, then tried to push him overboard," giggled Petra.

"So, she has lost her mobile, her iPad, and her purse. Was it worth it?"

"It was good of you to drop them off and come back and start the search. While they sort out their problem, it leaves us alone," she grinned.

"The least we could do. Hopefully, she has the

barbecue on for when we get back? Maybe she'll cook him well done," he laughed.

Bobby aided Petra to the back of the small cruiser. She threw her flippers on and heaved herself up, then collapsed back into the sea.

A cloud of murky red water surrounded her foot.

Petra froze rigidly. Fear overtook pain, shock overtook agony. Her foot was no longer there.

She screamed as she fought to scramble aboard. She looked back at her boyfriend, sinking helplessly.

"Oh, my God, Bobby," she mouthed as she watched him slowly disintegrate into popping bubbles.

Bobby's handsome features exploded into spumes of red jelly. Creatures were writhing inside his wetsuit, wrapping themselves along the anchor rope and crawling up and on towards her.

Petra slid towards the radio.

* * * * *

Mags sat motionless in the waiting room, staring ahead. She fixed her eyes on an unused hook on the wall.

"I wonder if it held a sign saying, 'beware of mad women,' or something similar? Oh, Robin, this is all my fault."

"Darling, please don't torture yourself. You are doing so well. This is certainly not because of you," said Robin.

"It's all my fault. If it wasn't for me, we wouldn't be here," mumbled Mags.

"Don't think like that. Are you okay there for a minute? I should check on the children again."

Her head bowed as she hugged herself, Robin stood slowly, touched her shoulder, and walked out.

"How are they, doctor?"

"We've removed all the... Uh, creatures. But had trouble stopping the bleeding, we've stitched them up, they appear fine now, but we must keep them in tonight. I want to find out what those things are," said the doctor.

* * * * *

"Sir, we have an SOS call."

"Put it on speaker," said the lifeboat skipper.

"It's mumbled now, strange because it was clear?"

The speaker crackled as if spitting threats.

"Trace that link, someone is in trouble," shouted the skipper.

We've lost it. I don't understand it?"

"What do you mean? Nothing?"
"Yes, Sir, silence."

"Get a chopper up there."

* * * * *

"We've got a fishing boat in our sights, we're going low for a closer look. It appears fine," said the helicopter captain.

"It looks like it's losing fuel. Look at the colour of the water," said his number two.

"There's nobody on deck. What is that? Look, the nets are moving."

"That is not netting, what the hell?"

"And all around the boat, sir, that is not oil."

"I can't go any closer. The oil, or whatever it is, is moving up and onto the deck. Where are the crew?"

"Christ, I hope that's fish blood?"

* * * * *

"Did you hear that?" asked Mags as she watched the hospital's overhead tv.

"Yes, the BBC told everyone not to go into the sea. What the hell?" Robin shook his head. He held out his arm to support his wife as he led her to the children's private rooms.

"Come on, Mags, do it for the children," he said.

"I should have stayed locked in the house. We all should have."

While they were wishing Jay and Lizzie a goodnight, a submarine slid into deeper water from nearby Portsmouth.

"We are approaching the site now, sir, port-side. You can see where the rocks tumbled deeper by the tanker that went down last week."

"The tanker finally got towed away, but leaving a hell of a mess?"

"Yes, sir, you can see the sludge that remains. They cleared most of it with high-powered jets of detergent. Wait a moment, what is that?"

"All engines stop, I want a closer look."

"Are those props from a sub? And that looks like a chunk of the rudder."

It puzzled the officers for a moment, then they spotted a smashed lump of steel.

"Bits of a submarine hull?"

"Is that the tower, over there?"

"Yes, sir. A wartime wreck, maybe?"

They radioed orders back and forth.

"Lieutenant, get us back. I've got a bad feeling about this," ordered the captain.

* * * * *

Senior officers had charts spread across an immense desk.

"Christ, look, the Admiral is already here," said the Lieutenant.

"Gentlemen. come in. What did you find?"

"Sir," said the Captain. "It appears to be a wartime sub, the rockfall must have disturbed its resting place," he smiled.

"This is no laughing matter!" growled the Admiral.

"No, Sir, sorry, Sir," said the Captain.

"Were there any identification marks on the hull?" asked the Admiral, looking at the Lieutenant.

"No, Sir, there wasn't much we could see. I guessed it was a wartime sub, judging by the rudder, Sir."

"No markings at all? How about the crew's skeletons?" asked the senior man.

"Not that we could see," the Captain scratched his chin, "any bones would have drifted away, surely?"

"What all of them?"

"Some rags were floating in the wreck, it could have been a uniform?"

"Get a diver there, we need to discover more."

The Admiral started searching through the wartime charts.

* * * * *

"We've lost the diver... Aargh!" screamed the divemaster, as he too became cloaked in black.

* * * * *

The Admiral was reading hand-written notes stashed in a file within a file. Brittle and dusty. 'Top Secret' stamped on it. 'Why was this never encrypted in computer files?' he thought.

"Christ, what is all this?" he breathed to himself.

"HMS Azur Lane? I've never heard of her? What the hell? Captained by Helex Robbo? Helex who? I've never heard of him. 'Sailed for a top-secret mission to destroy the Kaiserliche Marine', dated 1919."

The Admiral checked and reread more files, scratching and rubbing his jaw. He was none the wiser.

"What is this?" he opened a dusty envelope. "HMS Holland recommissioned, that cannot be?" He questioned the document. "It sank in 1913!"

Searching the dusty paperwork, "Renamed as Azur Lane, they sent it to German ports in the Baltic."

He read on. Sweat ran down his rigid jawline, "Armed with torpedoes packed with deadly germs!"

Search as he may, he failed to find a report on the details of the mission.

The Admiral collapsed back in his chair. Pouring himself a glass of rum, he downed it in one. He knew what he must do. He screwed the paperwork into balls, grabbing a wastepaper bin he filled it, then torched it on his desk. Embers turned to ash.

The 9mm pistol was still smoking as his secretary rushed to the door.

*Judge's Comments:* Another spooky story that left me not looking forward to my visit to the beach next week – ha ha! Very descriptive for a short story and certainly got the mind working over-time. Well written piece.

# OH, FOR GOD'S SAKE

## By LAWRENCE DRACUT
### Genre - Mystery

Yesterday morning I talked to God! I don't mean in the usual way that most people do, I wasn't kneeling by my bed praying, I just... talked to him.

I think?

I sat there at my desk as normal, coffee in front of me just wondering if I was going to start writing another novel, or maybe I should walk the dog as the sun was beckoning me to go outside. Any excuse to procrastinate. If there is a prize for that I would definitely win first place.

Suddenly I heard this commanding but calm and gentle voice from somewhere in the room, and before I could turn around to see where it was coming from, I was told to sit still and not speak for a moment. Strangely, I obeyed.

"I do not want you to be afraid," the voice said, "but I am the one you all call, God."

For some unknown reason, I remained calm and listened.

"Every thousand years or so the wife reminds me that I have to visit this planet and check on how you are all progressing. You know what's it's like to have a wife; better to do what they say and get it over with. So reluctantly here I am again."

By this time I had found my voice, daring to speak. "Why me, why did you pick me?" I stammered.

"Frankly, I didn't select you specifically, but she reminded me that on my last two visits I met with women. This time, she said that I should select someone who was about average, not very intelligent, and insignificant, so a man. You fit the requirements perfectly. I do not intend to be here for longer than necessary so let's get on with it. Ask what you want and I will try to answer in a way that your primal brain can understand."

Trying hard not to feel insulted I struggled to get my first question out, managing to utter, "If you only visit us once every thousand years, approximately, why this specific time?

"This will require a long answer so sit tight and wait for me to finish. I have been informed that you, and by you, I mean every human being on this planet, have made a total mess of things. I needed to see how badly and if the reports are accurate. Sadly, I can see that they are correct.

I remember when I first created this planet and what a beautiful place it was. I put all types of exotic and beautiful creatures on every continent and then caused wonderful trees and edible plants to grow equally. Also bushes with delicious fruit on them. They were there for the animals to eat but also wonderful to simply admire, such was their beauty. For eons, I was pleased and satisfied with my efforts.

However, after a few millennia had passed I must admit I was gullible enough to take advice from one of my most trusted helpers, those you call angels. His name was Yaldabaoth; you know him as Lucifer. He advised that as I didn't visit here very often, that may be all I had created should be enjoyed by some other type of life form. It seemed such a pity to waste it all on just the animals.

He said he could create others, suggesting that he introduce carnivorous animals. That they would keep the planet free of disease by eating the sickly, injured creatures and would ensure that the population was kept at a manageable level. I am afraid I agreed, instructing him to go ahead.

Considering that I am omnipotent I fell for all he said, even agreeing to his second suggestion. Commanding him to create mankind. That was probably the biggest mistake I have ever made. Especially as within just a few generations you started fighting and quarrelling with each other. You took possessions that did not belong to you, and even started killing animals for food. This really annoyed me since there was so much choice in the abundant vegetation. You have defiled paradise.

Do you know that I began to actually dislike you? I even thought about wiping you all off the planet completely and starting again. I will admit I did try out that plan on a small scale with a bit of a flood, but it made a mess of the landscape so I changed my mind.

Of course, it became clear after a while what my little angel of light wanted all along. He had become bored with being my trusted helper and wanted somewhere to call his own. Somewhere he could rule over and have fun with. So, when I discovered this, I threw him and his minions out of our heavenly abode, telling him he could never return as he had betrayed me.

I have so many other worlds to care for that I could no longer spend any more time here. I left him and this planet, vowing to return every thousand years to survey what had become of Lucifer and what was now his sole domain…"

"What do I call you?" I interrupted. "Every religion calls you by a different name; Yaweh, Jehovah, Elohim, Adonai, Allah, Shiva, Atten, and dozens more. Why did you start so many different religions?"

"This will require a somewhat longer answer, and it goes back to Lucifer again. It was not long before he had once more become bored. He had always been mean-spirited but by now he was becoming extremely bloodthirsty. It was getting more difficult to start wars, which seemed to be his favourite pastime. He had to think of new ways to entertain himself.

He had for several years persuaded one very large group of people to build this massive tower in a futile attempt to reach heaven. It wasn't possible of course; it was just his way of annoying me. Once this tower, you people called it Babel, was almost complete he, not me as many of you think, caused everyone who had worked on it to start speaking in dozens of different languages. It was absolute chaos. This seemed to appease his sense of humour.

Eventually, though he needed something else to keep himself occupied. It was then he formulated the most diabolical and destructive idea his malevolent mind could spawn. He created religion.

He had already disrupted the civilizations with his multi-language concept, so it was relatively easy to give mankind new beliefs and ideas, forcing these groups even further apart. To one tribe he would give certain commands and instructions, then totally different ones to another tribe, and so on and so on. Of course, each and every tribe were then convinced that their beliefs and way of life were the right ones.

Further, he commanded that they write it all down in various forms so it would carry on *religiously* forever. My little joke there! But to continue, several leaders were appointed to ensure that every command he gave them was adhered to as given them. These leaders called themselves prophets, which apparently gave them a sense of self-importance. But, here comes the best bit, and I have to admire his ingenuity for this, he said that all of this came from me.

Oh! I almost forgot to tell you. There were never any physical manifestations at all, ever, to anyone, anywhere. It was all accomplished through dreams or visions. Of course, mankind being a simple primitive life form listened to what they believed came from, God! Who could say it didn't. To deny that would be a punishable sin. I must say that was a brilliant move on his part.

So, for the next few thousand years, wars were fought, lands invaded, millions of people killed, and all in my name. Strangely, I don't even have a name. I am quite content to be known as, I AM, or the omnipotent one.

Of course, that meant he could tell them anything he wanted, always giving the instructions through a man, *my prophets!* He was probably the first misogynist? Or, maybe he just took advantage of the fact that most men are extremely gullible.

So, as everyone was now speaking a different language it was easy to tell one group this is God's name, that he has caused to be written in such a way, and this is how you should worship if you want to please him. Then he would go to a different tribe, give them a different name for me, and a different book of instruction. All for the purpose of furthering enmity between mankind. He must have enjoyed himself doing this.

Worst of all he even persuaded several of these groups to kill anyone that did not follow the same commands that had been written for them. They became so eager to please, that some even prayed to me, asking for help in their monstrous and mindless endeavours to slaughter any man, woman, or child that did not share their incredulous beliefs."

It was here that I became nervous for God had raised his voice. Not a lot, but enough for me to sense that he was angry. I will admit to a slight trembling of my entire body as he continued speaking.

"Why would I be pleased in the destruction of what I had caused to be created? I create, I do not destroy!" He calmed a little.

"But, to get back to you young man, it is time for me to leave. I think you have just enough intelligence to realise that currently there is a lot of work to be done on this world that you live in. I no longer have the patience, or desire to do anything about it or even talk about it.

However, I will shortly remove Lucifer and his followers from this place, and find a nice barren but habitable planet for them to live on. So, no more influence or interference from anyone. You will all be on your own. What happens next is entirely up to you and your fellow man, and woman, of course?

I will return in another millennium. It will be interesting to see if you have made any progress at all, or if there is even anything left of this once beautiful planet. I do hope there is something as I don't want to start over from scratch. Oh, by the way, you all have eternal souls, so make of that what you will!"

Abruptly I was once again on my own. My coffee had gone cold and the sun was beginning to set. I have no idea how long I had been sitting there. I do know that I felt troubled as I tried to make sense of the past lost hours. Had God actually spoken to me, or was I too having visions and dreams like the prophets of old. Or maybe I was having an episode of schizophrenia? It was all too much for my fragile mind to bear.

I decided to take the dog for a walk.

*Judges' Comments: This is certainly a different view on how God might look at the world of today and should make us all think about our future. Nicely worded and laid out. Well done.*

# IN TROUBLE AGAIN

## By MAUREEN EDWARDS

### Genre – Contemporary Fiction

*'In trouble again.'* Elaina Rubens read the text, then threw her phone down on the desk. He was such an embarrassment. Some days it did not pay to work in the same town she lived in. She had thought about moving so many times, especially after the first incident last month, but Elaina did not want to disrupt his entire life. Now it was *her* life in chaos. Constantly.

She looked at her calendar, trying to reschedule her appointments yet again, hoping her clients would understand. The houses would not sell themselves. Furiously she emailed a few clients to change some house visits - it worked out well this time. What a miracle! These high-net-worth customers had little time for shenanigans, and her life seemed full of that with him.

Owning Rubens Reality did have its perks. She could delegate a lot to some very talented people, but they knew. They all knew about him, and the constant issues he was having lately. Leaning on her desk, she stared out the window at the glorious old pussy willow swaying back and forth. She often wondered why the branches didn't break off and escape to freedom.

Gritting her teeth, foot bouncing up and down, she waited for the inevitable call when it happened. Windchimes tingled as her phone vibrated. She had changed her ringtone from fun, lively jazz music to a more tranquil sound, hoping it would keep her calm before the calls. The inevitable calls.

Cracking her neck, she recognized the number, clearing her throat ready to say, "Principal Calib, good morning!"

"Elaina, hey, it's Laura Mercer from guidance. We have a situation. If you can, please come over."

Her foot was jumping even faster now. "Laura, this is a surprise. I am confused. Usually it…"

"Not this time. I'll clear things up, but we need you here as soon as possible. You will be meeting with a group of us this time."

"Group? Should I be more worried than all the other times? Does it include the police again too?" Elaina whispered so as not to draw attention.

"How soon can you get here? We're getting everyone together now." Laura's voice was short and firm.

Elaina jumped up. "On my way. Do I need a lawyer again? We've known each other for a long time. I'd love a heads up. Don't think my heart can take it." Slamming down her laptop and almost knocking over her cup of water, her hand was shaking.

"See you in a bit." Laura Mercer ended the call.

Elaina stood for a moment, leaning on her desk. *'Dear God, please don't let them take him away from me. Good, bad, or what have you. Just keep him safe. No matter what.'*

She closed the door to her office and briskly walked past the other agents, waving and mouthing the words, 'See you later.' She tried pretending to be as calm as possible but her mouth was dry, her stomach in knots. Elaina stayed composed, almost until the very last step off the curb when her three-inch heel buckled slightly, causing her to stumble into the side mirror of her brand-new black Audi sportscar. It was a lease, but essential to keep up the illusion of prosperity, even though she struggled to even make the mortgage these days due to the rehab bills. It was always because of him. Shaking off the pain in her foot, she cursed under her breath. The last thing she needed was a hospital visit on top of whatever she was facing in the next few minutes.

She flopped into her front seat and grabbed the mint container. Anyone with half a brain would take a mint to turn the stale coffee breath into a minty jubilee. Elaina opened the container, and just as she was ready to pop one, she remembered her promise to her ex-husband to stay sober. These mints were never just mints, but uppers to help her get through the trials and tribulations of being the mother of a monster. Glassy-eyed, she resisted the temptation, especially since she would be in the presence of people who might see through the disguise.

Elaina texted her best friend: '*wish me luck,*' then turned on the car. Her friend always knew what that meant. She immediately got back the typical response which had saved her life, time and time again. It read: '*You got this*' before she had even moved the car. Taking deep breaths in and out, she drove the speed limit, whilst the radio blasted classic rock love songs. They reminded her of her ex-husband, the kindest man she had ever known. Song after song was like a kiss and a hug from him. Or had been when he had cherished and adored her.

Pulling up at the school, the visitor parking spot was open as usual. Chuckling, Elaina considered getting a sign with her name on it to reserve the spot. She was there so many times, she couldn't count anymore. Car off, she swished a little water from the bottle in her pocketbook and checked her tired image in the mirror. The last thing she needed, while facing the firing squad, was a bit of egg stuck in her teeth from breakfast. Dabbing on a bit of lipstick and spraying a spritz of perfume, she took one more look, straight into her piercing blue eyes. They were identical to his, which was a blessing when he was little, but now it was her curse.

Her foot ached from the near wipeout, but she hobbled into the school, her shoulders pushed back. She patted down her black pantsuit to ensure any wrinkle that dared to intrude was pushed away. She felt good about her look; it prepared for the new battle she was to face. She giggled as she heard the secretary buzz her in before she had even said her name to the speaker. What else is new? *I should get an office here.*

"Elaina, thanks for getting here so soon. We're in here," said Laura Mercer. She followed the preppy, perky, fit guidance counselor to a new location.

"No principal's office this time, Laura?" Elaina wobbled again.

Laura rubbed Elaina's shoulder. "Not today." And they walked in silence into the guidance suite. "One minute, please. Why don't you take a seat, and I will get him?"

Elaina chose to stand for a second but then thought otherwise. Looking at her foot, it was red and swollen, so she sat down, hoping she would be able to walk to the room from this point. She tried to camouflage herself into the background since the office was as busy as a subway station at rush hour. Several students sat in chairs waiting to discuss their college aspirations, domestic conflicts, or reasons for cutting class. Four secretaries were either pounding away at a computer or chatting on the phone. It was so busy she hoped no one had noticed or recognized her. But the glances from the adults in the room made Elaina paranoid. Time after time, she was the mother of **that kid**.

"Mrs. Rubens." Her name echoed as Laura's voice snapped her back to reality. The guidance room was full of new faces, except one. His. A fake smile. She followed Laura, a close friend with her until all these incidents had started last month.

Instead, she avoided his eyes and walked around the room as if it was a business meeting, shaking each person's hand, one by one, a sea of eight faces.

"Hello, I am Elaina Rubens." Mixed with, "Sorry about all this," and "Nice to meet you," or " I wish this was under better circumstances."

Elaina offered her hand to a young blond girl, a student, who needed prompting by the woman who looked exactly like her, except older, sitting next to her. "Go ahead, Mallory." And with that, Mallory offered her hand to Elaina. The grip was limp and sweaty. There was no nod. No eye contact.

*'Oh boy, what has he done to this girl?'*

Elaina sat down in the one empty seat next to him. Her image and likeness. Her flesh and blood, Xavier. He continued to look down. Elaina placed her fancy, expensive bag down and folded her hands, gripping them tight. She sniffed and could smell her perfume. *'Uh, way too much again. Nervous habit'.* She noticed the table was empty. No papers. No folders. No documents for her to sign. No suspension paperwork. No referrals for outside therapy. Nothing. Very weird.

Laura Mercer tilted her head, then cleared her throat, "Mrs. Rubens, thanks for coming so promptly. We all wanted to address the matter quickly between Mallory and Xavier, as it has been going on for some time. It has been the source of a lot of confusion for all of us."

Elaina shot Xavier a look, gritting her teeth. '*Dear God!*' Her face was getting flushed as if she had just been electrocuted. Both legs trembling, she could no longer feel the ankle she had twisted. She was numb.

"I wanted to hear Xavier's side and thought you should be here while he explains things." Laura lowered her head, attempting to get some eye contact. "Please talk to us, Xavier. I know you must be very upset. Mallory is too."

Elaina blurted out, "He doesn't talk to me much either. But I'm so sorry Xavier upset her. I'm so sorry! Is there anything I can do to fix this? Will you suspend him?" Elaina turned to him, face flush, "Xavier, what do you have to say for *yourself*?"

Xavier shrugged his shoulders. His pale cheeks turned a slight shade of pink as he stole a gaze at the girl. "Sorry, Mallory," he whispered.

Elaina moved her chair a little closer to Xavier's chair. "That's a start. Keep talking, buster."

Laura held her hands up, "Mrs. Ruben, he's not…"

Elaina cut her off, "We have been here before, young man." She was waving her finger in Xavier's face. "Fess up if you know what's good for you." Elaina's heart was racing.

Laura interrupted. "Mrs. Rubens. Please give Xavier a chance to explain!" Laura pulled out a manila envelope and slid it in front of Xavier. "Open it up."

Xavier placed his hand on the folder and pushed it away. Elaina pursed her lips. "Oh, for God's sake, Xavier, *for once in your life*!" Elaina cleared her throat, opened the envelope, and found tiny pieces of paper. Blinking quickly, she dumped the papers on the table. "What is this, Xavier? What have you done to poor Mallory!"

"No!" Mallory pounded her hands on the table. She covered her eyes and started to whimper.

Xavier looked at Mallory and, with the palms of his hands, said in a soft voice, "Calm down, Mallory. It's OK." Each word was intentional, like a doctor carefully examining a fragile patient. He nodded, as Mallory made eye contact with him. They both had a gentleness in their exchange as if Xavier was on a tightrope. Not too fast, not too slow, but very carefully.

Elaina shook her head and tapped her fingers on the table. "I'm confused." Taking one of the slips of paper Elaina opened it, and read it to herself. Gulping, she flattened the slip out, blinking back tears. She gasped. "Xavier... this is what Daddy told you all the time." Flattening the crinkled pages, slip-after-slip, she read the same message. Xavier and Mallory's eyes never left one another as the room remained silent. Elaina placed the notes one by one down a straight line. Twenty in total. All the exact phrases. *It's nice to be nice.*

Elaina moved a little closer to her son. "What's this, Xavier? Daddy always said this to you growing up."

Xavier licked his lips. "Mallory was mistreated every day! I did everything I could to help her, but I kept getting in trouble. So, I sent her these messages. We are friends. Secret friends. I wanted her to know I had her back!"

Laura leaned forward. "You should have come to us, Xavier. To a teacher. To your mom."

Xavier crossed his arms and rubbed them slowly. "I couldn't. Didn't want to be a snitch."

Laura shook her head. "But you have been blamed for so much, Xavier! Time and time again, you were suspended, given detention. We thought it was you bothering Mallory!" Laura sat back in her chair. "If Mallory's mom hadn't found these messages in her room, we wouldn't have realized you were the good guy in all this. We need names, Xavier. We have to undo all the weeks and months of making you the scapegoat."

Elaina put her hand on Xavier's hand. "I had no idea you had it in you. You're so quiet all the time. I know it's been hard since your dad moved out, and well, I've had my issues. You're more like him every day, in a good way."

Mallory nodded. "The best way. His sweet messages kept me going until today. Xavier, I'm sorry, but I don't want you in trouble anymore. It's not fair."

Laura pointed to three other adults in the room. "Xavier, these teachers are all here to support you. They were wrong to blame you for things when you were just trying to be a good friend to Mallory."

Elaina tightened her hand on that of her sons. He squeezed her back for the first time in a long time. Elaina's neck and face were reddening. "So, the nightmare of the last few weeks was just that. A setup! The other kids."

Laura nodded. "As we speak, the real culprits are being suspended. That's why Principal Calbi is not here right now. He has to undo much of what has been done. But Mallory, and Mallory's mom, wanted to meet with you both to say something. Right, Mallory?"

Mallory whispered, "Xavier, my mom, and my speech therapist helped me with this. She began reading. "I just got here a few months ago and have been tortured every day. Lunch, homeroom, gym, art, music. It's been terrible. They bully me on the computer, too. I have a hard time reading all the messages, but they post mean things. You are my only friend. Thank you for sticking up for me and putting these notes in my locker, even when you got into trouble. You're my only friend here, and I want to keep it that way. You're my best friend, Xavier."

As her smile lit up the room a tear fell from her mother's cheek. She mouthed the words "Thank you" to Xavier and nodded to Elaina.

Elaina leaned over and put her arm around Xavier, who was blushing. "We have a lot to discuss at home. I thought you were going to be like me but you are becoming more like your father every day. I'm so proud of you!" Elaina pointed to the slips of paper on the table. "Can I take one of these with me?"

Laura tilted her head and opened her arms wide. "As long as it's OK with Xavier and Mallory!"

Xavier and Mallory smiled at each other, and each pushed the messages '*It's nice to be nice*' towards every adult in the room, as they all waited for Principal Calbi.

*Judge's Comments: A story offering a view of loyalty, friendship, and support. This shows that not all kids are bad even when one might think they are. Perhaps another version of never 'judging a book by its cover.' A great read that many parents will be able to relate to.*

# KYLE'S TIME TRAVEL
## By GARIMA NABH
### Genre – Sci-Fi

*Washington D.C., 3020*

Kyle stepping out of his time machine, which he had named KYTE 1, he found himself surrounded by ruins much like the wastelands of the 21st century. Food containers, pieces of bottles, worn-out bags, and a robotic part that looked like the broken arm of a robot. Kyle carefully stepped around, picked up the item, and examined it. It seemed similar to the robots depicted in the Terminator series. He chuckled to himself. Perhaps the future isn't much different from what the movie showcased. Or is it?

Samantha, the AI of KYTE 1 spoke, "Doctor Kyle, what are you going to do now that you are in the future?"

He spoke into his watch, which served as a communicator, "I am interested in how the future will be. At least I can discover if I will be part of history."

Kyle felt proud of himself as the first person who had travelled to the future to witness his legacy. Of course, others had also tried but failed. He had first wanted to test his machine and possibly bring back evidence from the 31st century to prove himself. He wished to recreate history.

"You know that you can't stay long. You only have one day, otherwise, you will grow old fast and die before you can even go back to your own time," Samantha reminded him.

Yes, he knew it was necessary to stay only briefly. Despite his enthusiasm, he was anxious. What if he was arrested and never released? What if he got captured by aliens and experimented on? That's why he had his AI using his watch. Samantha could scan things for weaknesses or loopholes.

"I am not worried as long as I have you." Kyle glanced around to make sure no one was there before turning back to the machine. "Please shut the machine and start the timer."

"Good luck, doctor," the AI responded. The door of the machine shut with a click and a timer on the top of the door started like a ticking time bomb.

Kyle took a deep breath before moving forward. He hoped, to all that was holy, that his mission was going to be a success.

Moving around the debris, he had to cover his nose from the stench. Kyle gazed around while walking. The heat wasn't too much but still, sweat beads rolled down his forehead and oozed forth from other parts of his body. He removed the lab coat he had almost forgot he wore and slung it over his back.

As he continued walking, he spotted buildings in the distance. Shielding his eyes from the sun, he saw that the buildings were tall as if they touched the sky. Drawing nearer, Kyle heard sounds similar to that of airplanes and looked up. Alien-looking aircrafts moved about in the sky like seagulls over a river brimming with fish. They intrigued him. Was it going to be easier and faster to travel? Will man be able to fly to outer space, like in Star Trek?

As Kyle thought about all this, he reached a fence-like wall. He looked left and right but there was no one around. Checking for any security cameras he found none. It was strange that there was no guard around. Beyond the wall, he glimpsed the bustle of a city. A futuristic city. Wanting to get a closer look, he had to walk along the wall.

He was so distracted by the scenery in front of him that he didn't notice a child hovering nearby.

"Hey man, whatcha doing here?"

Kyle jumped and saw a boy on what looked like a skateboard that could float. He wore a worn-out suit that seemed to be big for his size. The type of clothes here were different. The boy looked curiously at him. Kyle straightened and prepared himself for the unknown.

"Are you deaf? Or are you mute? Because if you are then you deserve to be outside. People like you aren't needed."

Kyle realised the boy was about to leave.

"Wait!" he shouted.

The boy stopped and turned back to look at Kyle.

"How do I enter this place?"

"Don't you have your ID?"

"What ID?"

The boy looked at Kyle suspiciously. "Are you an outcast or criminal? Even those people can get fake IDs."

"I am neither." Kyle had to think hard and fast. He brightened as an idea struck. "I've lost my ID."

The boy continued eyeing him with suspicion. "What about your clothing? I have never seen those types of things."

Kyle looked down at himself. Crap. He hadn't thought so far. "It's...um… it's a costume. Yeah, I am posing as a 21st-century scientist." Kyle looked up at the boy with a big smile hoping to be convincing enough.

But the boy wasn't to be deterred.

"Costume? For what?" He straightened up, crossing his arms on his chest. The boy looked no more than eleven or twelve, yet tried his best to be intimidating.

"As I said, I lost my ID. I have memory issues, so I don't remember coming here. Maybe my friends dropped me here as a prank and I have now remembered I need to hurry back. So, if you could just cut to the chase and help me in. Please."

"And what do I get? If I am to help, you have to give me credit."

"Credit? What do you mean?"

Before the boy could answer, his flying skateboard lost its balance and he fell. The skateboard also fell having lost its power.

"Damn, I thought I got it fixed." Getting up, the boy brushed the dust from his suit and examined his skateboard. "The stupid fixer didn't do the work properly and cheated me just to get some credit."

Kyle squatted to the boy's level. "Hey, maybe I can help if you let me in. Then you wouldn't need to spend more credit."

"What's in it for you? And how do I know you won't cheat me."

Kyle sighed, getting frustrated, but he needed to be patient if he wanted to be in and out of here on time.

"Look kid, we can help each other. I will help you so that your skateboard will be as good as new, and you won't need to spend more credit. In return, you need to help me get in and help me with a new ID. Deal."

The kid looked him up and down. "We would probably need to get you more than an ID… Deal. My name is Scott."

"Hi again. I'm Kyle."

Scott looked around warily first before producing his ID from an invisible pocket in his suit. Then he also brought out another card which prompted Kyle to think, that if people had to use only one ID card, what was the other one for?

As if reading his thoughts, Scott said, "Don't worry, the other card isn't illegal," he turned to Kyle with a sly smile, "it's just stolen."

Kyle could only stare at the young boy's confidence and bravery. He did not want to find out whose card it was or why Scott had stolen it.

The young boy placed the two cards at the same time into the fence and they disappeared into an invisible wall. There was a click and that part of the fence opened.

"Come on man, it's open for only 30 secs," Scott said, evidently getting impatient.

Kyle raced through to the other side, turning back in time to see the fence reappear as it was and the cards back in Scott's hand.

"Thanks for helping me."

They shook hands and Kyle picked up the skateboard and examined it. The equipment attached to the bottom of the skateboard resembled a mini aircraft engine. As Kyle set about fixing the equipment, he started asking Scott questions as innocently as possible.

Kyle learned that in the future a great meteorite crashed on Earth, specifically in America. It contained alien elements which had been harnessed to develop better technology. Then the American leaders had waged war on other countries until gradually they ruled the whole world. Just like when the Europeans colonised the world. No one had been able to fully understand the meteorite or its elements.

After fixing the skateboard, Scott took him to a nearby rural area. It wasn't much different than in the 21st century. The place was filthy and populated with poor people and beggars. They stared at Kyle as if he were an alien. Well, he supposed he was in a way because he didn't belong there. After going through a long alley, Scott stopped at a door.

Before knocking, he spoke. "Now, don't say a word. Better let me handle this."

Kyle nodded, grateful for the young boy's help. If not for Scott, anything could have happened to him. So using the universal sign of keeping quiet, Kyle zipped his lips.

Scott chuckled. "You really are a fast learner."

He knocked on the door twice. It was opened by a big burly man, fit to be a bouncer of a nightclub. He eyed Kyle while Scott talked to him in hushed tones. Eventually, the man nodded and allowed them both to enter, locking the door behind them.

Kyle looked around to see people on computers. He guessed it was an illegal computer center. Ever since the computer had been built, and especially since the digital age, the internet had become one of the weapons for criminals to use. Hacking accounts, frauds, and thefts of computer hardware and software became prominent. However, in this case, he had no option but to go along with it. All this time, he had forgotten about Samantha. He checked his watch and noted he had already spent two hours.

Time Remaining 22 hours.

He knew his AI was recording everything. Smart one at that. This would be some evidence. He saw

Scott talking to a man. The man was listening to the kid but his eyes were on Kyle. He felt uneasy as if something bad was going to happen. The man's eyes widened as if in recognition and suddenly stood up making Scott jump back in surprise.

"I have been waiting for you."

Kyle looked around to see who the strange man was talking to, but there was no one. The people in the room stopped working and watched them. The man's eyes bore into Kyle's.

"I know who you are and why you are here."

Scott looked between both of them, confused.

"Hey man. You know him?"

"Yes," his only answer.

Kyle gulped, afraid to say anything.

"Cat got your tongue?" The man looked at him in amusement. "You are Professor Kyle Bane."

Kyle spluttered, "What the hell! How do you know?"

The man laughed. "He talks."

Some people in the room laughed, while others gave curious glances as if it was the most entertaining thing of the day.

The man turned to the others in the room, suddenly serious. "All right people. Back to work."

They all obediently turned back to their computers, although Kyle could see they still were watching them surreptitiously.

Scott looked at the man in confusion. "What's this all about?"

The man turned. "You will see. Follow me."

He turned and walked away down a nearby corridor without waiting to see if they would follow. Kyle and Scott were so stunned it took them some time before they also started moving.

"Who is he?" Kyle asked in a whisper.

"You'll find out." Scott looked at him suspiciously. "If you aren't who you say you are, then you're in trouble buddy and there's no way I can help you out of this."

The man was waiting for them by an open door. "Get inside quickly."

Kyle entered a small room that had a bench, a chair, and a table on which was a computer. Both of them sat on the bench while the man sat on the chair facing Kyle.

"I am sorry. I forgot to introduce myself. I never thought that I would meet you, so you shocked me. It took me some time to recognise you."

"This is the first time I have come here. How can you know me?"

"Because," the man leaned closer. "I am your descendant."

"What!" Scott shouted. "How's this possible? This dude lives here. How can you be his descendant?"

The man leaned back in his chair. "No. This dude is from the 21st century. He's my so many times great grandfather. Isn't that right?"

Kyle, shocked into silence, didn't know whether to shout in joy at meeting his future family or to be scared of the knowledge of the future. Aware that any changes in time travel can alter the future timeline, the question was how did this man know him? And, why did he say he has been waiting for him.?

"What's your name?" Kyle finally asked.

"David. I am assuming you want to ask what I know."

Kyle nodded mutely.

David turned to the computer and started typing.

"I know Scott has told you about the meteorite containing the elements which crashed in America. However, he doesn't know everything." David turned the computer for the two of them to see.

An article dated 2045 appeared on the screen. A picture of the meteorite crash landing on earth. There was also a picture of Kyle, the head of the research team who first studied the meteorite.

"Wow!" Scott said in amazement. "So, it is true?"

David turned back the computer and typed again.

"Despite the fact you were the head of the research team, the American government didn't give you credit for your work. Also, they later labelled you as a traitor to the country."

"What? Why would I be a traitor?" asked Kyle in shock.

"Because," David again turned the computer to show another article. "You steal a part of the meteor and sell it to America's enemies. When you are found guilty and persecuted, you tried to run away but were captured, spending the rest of your life in prison."

Kyle read the article. Not once, not twice but thrice. He read about his parents, wife, and children all of whom had suffered due to his future actions. They became a target of mockery. His wife, not able to tolerate being a traitor's wife, had committed suicide. His parents had moved to the countryside with his children to avoid media attention.

But it still didn't answer, how did David know that Kyle would come to the future?

"How did you know about me coming to the 31st century?"

David pointed to his watch. "Samantha. Your AI. Isn't she recording everything?"

To make sure it was working, he spoke as calmly as possible. "You there Samantha?"

"Yes, doctor."

Kyle looked at David. "But how?" he asked in a voice so small, it was almost a whisper.

"You gave the watch to your father for safekeeping. After you were taken to jail, your father listened to the recordings, unable to believe his only son could be treasonous. That knowledge had been passed down through the generations until it came to me."

David leaned closer to his ancestor. "Even after you and your parents' deaths, the world still believes that we all are traitors. We have been watched closely both by the media and the governments because your actions not only threatened this country but the whole world. Now only you can change the future if you so wish."

The whole time Scott hadn't said anything. Kyle couldn't blame him. He could see the evidence right in front of him, and the knowledge that David was aware of his past actions.

"He's right, doctor," said Samantha, breaking the silence. "According to my calculations, there's still time to avoid the catastrophe that would descend on your family."

This was not what he expected. This wasn't how he wanted to be remembered. Being a traitor of his country, and his family suffering the consequences of his actions. Making up his mind, Kyle stood up. At the same time, David and Scott also stood.

"Thank you," said Kyle although he wanted to, he refrained from saying, my son. Instead, he enveloped David in a big bear hug. Stunned, David stood for some time before wrapping his arms around his ancestor. After that Kyle turned to Scott and hugged him as well.

"Thank you, also. You have been a good companion. Although my time here has been very short, I have learned something important, and…" he turned to David, "…I promise not to let any harm come to our family."

The two relatives, one from the past and one from the future looked at each other. It was as if they had come to an unspoken understanding. David and Scott quietly led Kyle back to his time machine, each lost in their thoughts.

Kyle, who had initially been ecstatic about his invention and travelling to the future, now forgot his mission of taking back evidence of time travel. After passing through the fenced wall, he led them to his time machine. Although it looked primitive to the future generations, for him it was the greatest invention of his life. Turning back to look at the future for the last time, Kyle saw the sun setting on the horizon. It was beautiful.

"Well, this is it."

Ordering Samantha to open the door, he entered the machine. His throat being choked with emotion meant he couldn't do anything but wave.

Eventually, Samantha spoke, "It was nice meeting you, David and Scott. Hopefully, you will meet me in the future."

For the first time, David smiled, while Scott had tears in his eyes.

"Goodbye, buddy," he said.

"Goodbye, Scott."

Kyle looked at David for the last time. "Please take care of Scott."

"Will do," David said.

As soon as the door closed, Kyle started the machine to take him back to the past where he belonged. He was going to rectify the mistake he was supposed to make before it happened.

**Judge's Comments:** An interesting story, well written for someone whose first language is not English. This story could be developed into a longer novel, perhaps by including many more adventures. Good read.

# HABITS DIE HARD

## By MAUREEN EDWARDS

## Genre – Contemporary Fiction

As Ed paced his small studio apartment, limping slightly, his hands were shaking, palms moist. The sun glistened through the window but didn't illuminate the space enough to bring a smile to his face. The loneliness and sorrow of the last six months paralyzed him. Fresh air was not welcome. Isolation was his best companion. The bullet lodged in his neck ached like his broken heart and shattered dreams. One day bled into a week, which bled into a month.

*'Nothing cheers me up,' he thought.*

As always around this time, the door down the hallway slammed. Darting to the door like a feeble deer, he softly laid his head against the wood, tightly gripping the doorknob. The two sets of footsteps were deliberate - one large set of clomping shoes and one tiny pair of tiptoe sneakers. He knew from weeks of reconnaissance that his neighbors, a mother, and child, were going out for a stroll. He stood frozen until he heard the elevator doors close.

*All clear.*

Stuck in his spot for a minute, he closed his eyes and counted to ten. Finally, Ed loosened his grip on the doorknob to look at his watch. Twelve hundred hours meant lunch. He yawned, exhausted from the side effects of the new medication.

He flopped on the couch for a nap. There were no sweet dreams for Ed, just planes taking off and never landing. Eyes closed, body tense, he drifted off into hell.

He buckled himself into the middle seat of the plane. To his left, a bloody leg, to the right a faceless young boy. Beads of sweat rolled down his face as he frantically searched in his duffle bag for band-aids, tissues, something to help! But there was nothing.

Next, he looked to his left and saw a tiny dead infant without limbs. Heart racing, he looked to the right, seeing his mother staring back at him, crying, reaching for his hand. Nearly touching her fingertips for a caress, loud music startled him from his nightmare. He sat up in a pool of sweat, tears in his eyes, as his cell phone ring tone rang out Queen's, 'We Will Rock You'. Disoriented, he jumped off the couch and stood to attention. Swallowing hard, Ed recognized his small, empty, cold apartment. Grabbing the phone, he shook his head. *No one called. Ever.* Unless it was Lt. Harris. And it was.

"Did I catch you at a bad time?" Lt. Harris's voice was calming to Ed.

The dark rings under Ed's eyes were a sharp contrast to his pale white skin that had not seen the outdoors in weeks. He pushed his hand through his high, tight haircut. "Just another day, sir."

"I've some good news for you. You sitting down?" Lt. Harris sounded cheery.

Shrugging, Ed sat down since he always followed commands. "Now I am, Sir."

"I spoke with the dog breeder last night. I know it's been months, and we haven't talked about it in a while, but you've got one! Do you know how hard it is to get a service dog?"

Ed raised his eyebrows and rubbed his stubbly chin. His voice was monotone. "It's great to hear, Sir. When?"

"Soon. It can never replace Boxer, you know. Do you wanna talk a little now? How ya feeling?"

An ambulance passed by the apartment with sirens blaring. Ed jumped up, hobbled over to the side of the glass window, and slowly glanced out, teeth clenched.

Lt. Harris called out from the phone. "Ed! I hear the ambulance. Talk to me."

With laser focus, Ed looked around and said, "All clear, sir."

"Good. How's the new medicine?" Lt. Harris sighed, "You sleeping?"

Ed lied. "Yup. Big difference, Sir."

Lt. Harris calmly said, "Not sure about that, since we just switched again. Listen, any word from your family? Your daughter, Beth?"

He lied. "Yea, she's doing good, Sir."

"Good. You were going to talk to Beth about maybe moving in with her. She lives on a quiet block, you said. How about food? You shopping? You have enough?"

Ed walked into the kitchen, opening up the bare cabinet door. "Yup. All good, Sir."

"Stay strong, Ed. Things will get better once you look for a new place. Talk soon," and Lt. Harris ended the call.

Ed glanced at his opened laptop, seeing all his unanswered emails from Beth. *Living with her and the baby might be good?* Rubbing his chin, he shut the machine fast as his heart began to race. *She can't see me like this. I don't want to be a burden.*

Entering the kitchen, Ed splashed water from the sink onto his face, hoping he would wake up a bit. The brain fog from the medication would take time. He was well-used to that by now. He took out the moldy white bread, the expired peanut butter, and the cracked jar of jelly. And his favorite part of lunch - the knife!

He held the blade up to the light, examining it closely. Its edge was perfect since he sharpened all his knives every night after dinner. He could see his lifeless reflection. He breathed easier, holding it. Ed's mouth watered as he fixated on the blade. The vivid memories appeared. Ear-deafening gunshots, skin-burning flames, gut-wrenching screams, pungent-smelling odor. Shaking his head back to reality, he wiped the drool from his chin.

A fire truck roared by, and Ed jumped into action.

He was running back to the living room window again, clutching the knife to the side of his leg. He peeked out the window, scanning up and down the block. He gasped for air as if he had run a marathon.

*All clear.*

Leaning his head back against the wall, Ed closed his eyes for several seconds and counted. When he opened his eyes, he forgot where he was. Looking down at the knife, he took a deep breath in then strolled back to the kitchen.

Putting the knife in the jar of peanut butter, he slowly and carefully spread it on the bread. Next, he dipped it in the jelly. He swirled the red raspberry preserves around and around to smell the sweetness. He spread the jelly, like an artist painting a canvas. Placing the knife in his mouth to lick, he cut his tongue with the blade. This was habit now. The taste of his blood was savory. He pressed the bread together, took the knife out of his mouth, and sliced the sandwich almost like a surgeon.

*Perfection.*

He placed the knife in the sink as if it was a delicate piece of crystal. Just then, another siren roared past the apartment; this was the perils of living on a block with a hospital. Ed dropped to the floor face down, covering his head, eyes tightly shut. Hands shaking, heart pounding, face reddening, he waited until the sirens were silent once more. Moments later, he raised himself off the floor, picked up the sandwich, and threw it in the garbage. He could taste the bile from his fear in his mouth.

He leaned into the sink and stared at the knife. *Ah, what things I could do with that knife today.* Closing his eyes, memories flashed back. *He was cutting he throat of an enemy prisoner, stabbing the heart of a wild boar, severing the finger of a trapped officer, thrusting it in the chest of a charging guerilla.* He shook his head violently, bringing himself back to reality.

Dragging himself to the couch, Ed lay down, feeling exhausted. Before he knew it, he was dreaming of another plane, another seatbelt, and another lift-off, all the while clenching the armrests. He rolled over and over on the couch, moaning with fear until he heard an unfamiliar bang on the door. Sitting up his eyes were bulging.

*It has to be a mistake - enemy approaching.*

Ed reached under the sofa cushion, touching his cold metal weapon, and pulled it out gently.

*Who the hell was it? No one knocks on my door.*

He held the gun close to his chest, cradling it like a baby, caressing the side of the barrel.

The second knock was a faint, light tap. Ed waited, frozen in his spot as if he was in a foxhole.

The third knock was intense as if it was a fist-pounding.

*They're not going to go away.*

Ed stood up slowly, pointing the gun at the door with his right hand while wiping his left hand on his pants. His mouth was dry. He tried to speak, but no words came out.

The fourth knock was more like a bang. He tiptoed to the peek hole. He peered through it, forgetting he had put masking tape on the outside. He did not want anyone - the enemy, the government - to find him.

*I want to be left alone. No more fights, no more battles, no more blood, no more war.*

Ed put his ear against the door to listen. He nearly jumped out of his skin at the fifth knock. Body against the wall next to the door, gun held up, he tried to speak. This time he said in a loud voice, "Who is it?" He held the grip so tight his hand was turning purple.

"I was told Ed Smith lives here. Delivery." Her voice was husky.

Ed swallowed hard. "Leave it and go. I'll get it when you leave."

She raised her voice. "Sorry, man, it does not work that way. I need to hand-deliver it to you."

Ed slowly shoved the gun into the back of his jeans, freeing up both hands, but leaving the gun in easy reach if he needed it. "I don't know anyone who would send me anything."

"Well, I found you, so open up and get it. I'm not leaving until you open the door."

Ed unlocked the three bolts on the door with his left hand while his right hand was on the gun. He opened the door slowly to lock eyes with the glistening brown eyes of a chocolate Labrador. Letting go of the weapon slowly, his lips formed a slight smile.

The tall, muscular woman holding the leash, said, "I'm Rita, the dog trainer. It's your lucky day. Meet Champ."

Ed's eyes welled up, as he bent down to the eye level of Champ, petting his head. He whispered, "Champ."

The dog moved nearer, rubbing his face on Ed's neck where the bullet remained. Ed continued to pet the dog, smelling his perfumed coat.

*It's been so long.*

Rita held the leash and saw Ed's gun. Swallowing hard, she suggested, "Maybe you want to invite us in?" Her ripped jeans were tight around her middle, almost looking as if they would split if she sneezed. Her yellow neon shirt, which read 'United Rescue Dogs,' was so bright it could have been seen from Mars.

Ed stood up, wiped away a tear, and opened the door wider. This was the first time he had had company. As Ed walked over to the couch to place the gun back under the cushion, Rita and Champ stood in the center of the room.

Rita bit her lip. "Err... You might consider keeping that locked up someplace safe with Champ here." She popped a piece of gum from her pocket, chewing it with her mouth open. Her greasy black hair was pulled back in a messy ponytail.

He cleared his throat and looked around, "I... never thought about another place for it before... I will, ma'am."

Rita gave him the leash. "I can come and be with you a few times to go over how to work with Champ, but he's all yours! I was told you had a pretty free schedule."

Just then, a police car roared by. Ed dropped the leash and moved to the side of the window, peeking out. Champ followed him. Ed looked down, confused, distracted from the siren, as he smiled slightly to pet the dog. The knots in his back loosened, his heart rate lessened. "Good job, Champ."

Calmly Ed closed his eyes, took a deep breath, and opened them to see Rita's head tilted to one side. Her smile was broad. "This is why I do what I do, Ed. It's moments like this. A new life of hope. I just saw it all over your face."

Ed bent down and pet the dog again. "Please, ma'am, sit down. I'm sorry if I've been so..."

She placed a duffle bag down next to the chair. "Can I have a glass of water? It's brutal in here. It's safe to open a window, Ed." Rita walked over and opened the window to let in the cool fall air. The breeze blew the curtains slightly.

Ed blushed. "Of course, ma'am. Cold water, I promise." Walking into the kitchen, Champ followed Ed automatically. Taking out a glass from the cabinet he ran the water for a few seconds. Ed looked down at Champ, and Champ looked up at Ed. Having filled the glass he froze for a second as he saw the knife. He closed his eyes. *Blood. Guns. Flames.*

Rita's voice interrupted his trance. "I'll work with you and Champ and your schedule. I can tell you'll do great together! First, we are going to work on obedience and commands. It'll take a few weeks, but we'll become fast friends, I can tell!"

Ed did not give the knife a second thought; instead, he focused all his attention on Champ. Ed and Champ walked into the living room side by side.

'Wow, fresh air!' He handed the cold glass of water to Rita. 'I never noticed how bright this apartment is!'

Rita guzzled the water then placed the glass on the table. "How about I come back later so you can bond with Champ for a bit? There are some things for Champ in the duffle bag to get you started. Toys, food," and standing up, Rita walked to the door. Opening it she turned to see Ed sitting on the couch petting Champ. "Ed, when I knock in about an hour, it's safe. It'll just be me. How about I text you first with a five-minute warning? It will take a little time, but I can see Champ already likes you!" She chuckled, wiping some sweat away from under her eyes. "See you in a bit!"

Ed raised his hand to wave. "Will do, ma'am."

Having watched the door close behind her, his gaze immediately turned to the strange large, bulky duffle bag. He sat to attention in the chair.

Search it ASAP. Timer. Wires. Detonator. Ball bearings. Nails. Switch.

Slowly Ed reached under the cushion, took out the gun, and gulped hard. He brought the barrel of the gun closer and closer to his mouth, licking the muzzle.

Ah, the adrenaline rush.

This was habit now. Champ stood still, tongue hanging out of his mouth, panting fast. Ed locked eyes with Champ, took the gun out of his mouth, and pointed it straight at Champ.

Who are you, really? Why are you here?

Just then, a police siren roared by the apartment. Champ barked twice, snapping Ed out of his hypnotic state. Ed slowly lowered the gun and placed it on his lap. He glanced at the laptop with his unopened emails. Opening one from Beth, he read her sweet, tender words, bringing tears to his eyes. They rolled down his face as Champ moved closer to him. Sobbing, Ed stroked and caressed his faithful old companion with one hand, caressing his new protective acquaintance with the other.

*Judge's Comments: This is a very poignant story. And also quite graphic. One is truly led to believe the trauma that a veteran of war must go through once they return home. And the hope and relief that an animal can bring them. A well-written piece - not for the faint-hearted*

# WAITING TO BE COLLECTED

## By Dorit Oliver-Wolff BEM

## Genre – Contemporary Fiction

Betty's eyes were firmly fixed on the footpath that led to the front door of *The Happy Valley Residential Home for the Elderly*.

Her big chair was placed near the window, as it always was. This was BETTY'S CHAIR! No one, but no one, was ever permitted to sit in it. Never, ever.

MY CHAIR, MY PLACE. All residents had a personal chair and it was taboo to sit in anyone else's chair. Residents had had bitter fights over THEIR chair – even physical fights with the perpetrator if anyone dared to use the wrong chair.

The chair was the only thing that the resident could call their own – MY chair.

Betty was a small, immaculately clean, frail lady. She liked her clothes to be colour coded, to match her white hair. She had a perm every six weeks, and her toe and fingernails were manicured at the same time. Betty was friendly – but not too friendly. She didn't want to get too close to the others. She liked to exchange small talk but believed she was only there for a short time, so didn't want to get too involved or make friends during her short stay in the residential home.

Betty had six grown-up children. Her husband, Charlie, had been in the Army and was killed during the Second World War. Her eldest son, Fred, had been 14 and the youngest, Charlie Junior, was just two years old. She also had four daughters, Margaret (Maggie for short), Mary, Doris and Kate.

She married Charlie when she was just 18 years old and he was 22. Charlie had had a good job as a local postman, being paid regular wages but he also worked at the local butcher shop in the afternoon. This gave them a good income so they could put down a deposit on a small cottage with a small garden where Betty had planted plenty of vegetables. She had also kept two hens which gave them fresh eggs every day.

Betty busied herself knitting baby clothes and preparing for the big day when Fred would arrive.

She had been an excellent cook and could bake too, which she had learnt from her mother's sister, Ellie, who had brought Betty up, as her mother died when she was just 10 years old.

Betty had three older brothers who were each taken in by different members of the family, all over the country. They had, unfortunately, all lost touch.

Not much was known about Betty's father. Every time she had asked Auntie Ellie about him she was told, "Best not to mention him. He was no good. My poor sister; she had to bring up you and three hungry boys all on her own. Your Mum went into service and they provided a small cottage on the grounds. That is where she looked after you lot."

Auntie Ellie was kind to Betty. She had never had any children of her own. Her husband, Tom, was a clerk in a factory so they were quite well off. Betty learnt all she needed to know about how to bring up a family from Ellie.

As she grew up, Betty went to school and became a nurse. She was petite with dark brown hair and dark brown eyes. She was also an accomplished seamstress, making her own clothes. This came in handy when she moved into her first home as she made all the curtains and covers for the furniture. She even clothed her daughters, which she enjoyed doing.

When the war ended, and Charlie sadly didn't return, she had a small Widow's Pension from the

Army. The children went to local schools and thankfully, stayed out of trouble, which made life easier as it is very difficult to bring up six children without a father.

After the children left home, Betty went back to nursing in a local hospital. This meant that she could keep her little cottage, which she loved, as the mortgage had been paid off and she could afford to live comfortably. Her children and grandchildren would visit her regularly; and at Christmas and Easter, she always had a full house, which reminded her of the times when they were all living happily together.

All the children had good jobs and had married well so they were all independent and financially secure. Except that is, for Charlie Junior, who found it difficult to manage on the commission he received as an estate agent. His wife worked as a waitress and they had two teenage boys. But Charlie was a very loving son, who would pop in regularly to see his Mum for a cuppa.

Betty was now 86 years old, fit for her age and still active. Charlie had suggested that she should sell her little cottage so he could buy a bigger house where she could have her own accommodation but still be part of the family. 'This would make sense,' he had told her, as he would make sure that she would be looked after as she got older when she might need help.

The rest of the family had agreed that this was a good idea, mainly because most of them lived too far away to help if needed. And so, Betty agreed to sell her beautiful little cottage and it was sold within no time at all.

There was a delay with the purchase of the house that Charlie and his wife wanted to buy, so they all agreed that Betty would go into a residential home until the house was ready for them all to move into. Betty had a basic room in the home which she didn't mind as this was supposed to be for just a few weeks.

Charlie would come regularly to visit her, checking with her about what kind of decorations she wanted in her part of the house. He brought the house plan in which she would constantly show everybody, telling them how lucky she felt to be moving in with her son and his family.

Betty had positioned herself in her favourite chair, as usual. Her eyes were fixed on the footpath to the front door. She was waiting for Charlie to appear but all she got was a message from one of the carers, saying that Charlie was sorry but he couldn't come today because he was too busy.

Days turned into weeks, weeks turned into months. Even the telephone messages seemed to have stopped.

As time passed, everyone noticed that Betty had lost the spring in her step.

Many months had passed, so many that Betty had stopped counting. It could even be years by now.

She often fell asleep in her chair after her eyes became heavy from looking into the distance, hoping to see Charlie coming down the path again.

When people asked her how she was, her reply would always be, "Fine. I'm waiting to be collected."

*Judge's Comments: A true-to-life story of modern society and the unscrupulous people that unfortunately exist in this world of ours. One has to feel great sorrow for Betty. Well-written piece with a lot of feeling and explanation within it. Well done.*

# THE FAT LADY IS SINGING
## BY LAWRENCE DRACUT
### Genre – Contemporary Fiction

This is the first entry in a journal that will document the beginning of a new, but also the final chapter of my life.

My name is Henry Long, and tomorrow, the 28th of September 2047, is my seventieth birthday. My son and his family will hopefully be able to visit me. I am of course anxiously looking forward to seeing them.

However, it will also be the last time I see them until my next birthday, as on the 29th I will be moving from my current home, to UK region twelve, the same as many others my age who have miraculously survived the past decade, have. I will be collected by someone from one of the relocation agencies and taken to my new home.

I will explain why this is necessary later in the journal.

The new accommodation provided will, I have no doubt, meet the basic requirements for senior citizens, as established by the national security federation. I remember an old television sitcom where the presenter pointed to a large block of flats, humorously saying, 'and this is where we store our old people.' Unfortunately, that has now become a frightening reality.

Sometimes, I sit back and reflect on how we, a so-called civilized society, arrived at the situation our planet is now in. Long ago, I concluded that we were never actually civilized at all. We simply progressed. Driven forward by our petty wants and imagined needs.

It was over thirty years ago that several popular, educated, and well-informed individuals tried desperately for most of their lives, to make the world aware of the self-destructive path we had made for ourselves. Publicly they were applauded, being lavishly praised by mainstream media and governments alike. In reality, they were ignored whilst our lives carried on as normal, at least for a while.

Often I find myself laughing quietly at some of the past news programs proudly announcing, that after years of intense study, governments were making it illegal to provide and use plastic disposable shopping bags. Sadly this seemed to appease the general public. Doing this will help solve our entire environmental problem.

Really? Were we that stupid and gullible?

Yes, I am afraid we were.

I try with great difficulty not to reflect on the past, but try to recall all I can, recording it here. I do not want our grandchildren to be misled into thinking that they were in any way able to prevent the destruction of our planet and society as it was. It is solely the fault of my generation, and some of those before us.

It would be wrong of me to pinpoint to a specific individual, company or government as the sole cause, but rather it was a tsunami of global events. Irreversible climate change was upon us. We had gone too far, way past the point of return.

We had become a society that believed it was our right to have anything we wanted, and when we wanted it. We also became lazy consumers. At the push of a few buttons, our cravings were delivered overnight to our doorstep. No thought was given to the origin or construction of our purchase, or indeed the environmental damage its production had caused. Major appliances were made to be obsolete within five years, with only some parts being recycled. The rest was added to the landfill. The water and air pollution generated by the manufacture of products, clothing, etc., was something we did not consider, or worse, even care about. And yet we ploughed on.

Countries that were once considered poor, practically overnight become wealthy, due to their cheap labour force, and with total disregard for the environmental dangers. Thousands of factories polluted the rivers and oceans with their poisonous by-products. I recall with sadness a video taken in an Asian country, showing trucks lining up on a dock waiting to dump all their toxic garbage directly into the ocean.

Air quality became noxious, with the wearing of masks needed to prevent lung damage.

Warnings of climate change were continually rejected and even ridiculed until eventually they could no longer be ignored. The Antarctic ice sheet melted faster than even scientists thought possible, causing sea levels to rise, and coastal cities around the world to be submerged.

By this time, the pollution and dramatic change in weather patterns were causing a myriad of disasters. Floods, landslides, earthquakes and typhoons were becoming commonplace. Wildfires, that previously had only happened during the summer months, were now a regular occurrence, scorching thousands of square miles of land and destroying wildlife on every continent. Extreme weather was commonplace and unpredictable.

Space exploration continued.

I thought at first it was a search for another planet that we could inhabit, but eventually, the real reason surfaced. Mars, thought to be our new home once the destruction of this one became inevitable was, in reality, only investigated for the sole purpose of mining minerals that were needed in the manufacture of many of our consumer goods. Unbelievably amid the problems facing us, the need to produce consumer goods was still paramount.

I should mention that my timeline of events is not necessarily in the correct order as many overlapped. It is only important to note that they happened.

Ironically, many of the industrial leaders that were complicit in establishing our *progressive* society, were now being consulted by our governments in solving some of the problems they had helped create.

I don't know if you have ever read the definition of a Technocrat or Megalomaniac, but the former is a person who is a technical expert and wields great power and influence with both industry and governments. The latter, and to me the scariest, the Megalomaniac, has the drive to control people, has a sense of greatness, believing they are omnipotent. It is actually classed as a severe mental illness. It is to these individuals that we turned for help. Why not have the fox guarding the henhouse?

Oceans, so full of plastic combined with an increase in water temperature, killed most of the marine life. Once fertile soil dried up into barren wastelands. Animals died due to lack of vegetation, drinking water, and extreme heat. Food for man and beast alike became scarce. Entire nations on several continents died of starvation.

As if these disasters were not enough to cope with, very few countries escaped the emerging new plague-like viruses. The origins of which I am unsure. Natural, manmade or both? There was too much misinformation for me to speculate on the true source, although I have my suspicions. Still, we ploughed on.

Within only a decade, the planet's population was reduced to about two billion souls! There were, of course, pockets of civilization that survived. Parts of the UK, New Zealand, Iceland, the central plains of

America, and a few remote small islands. It was these countries that, for a brief time, were to experience the mass migration of refugees.

Sadly, many of those landing on coastal areas were met by hostile vigilante groups that repelled their attempts to reach land. Most were seen as invaders, not refugees. Extreme violence now seemed acceptable, often used by the self-appointed guardians of their homelands. Humanity no longer had a place in the tattered remains of society.

With only makeshift governments now in existence, numerous attempts were made to try and hold society together. They all failed. The introduction of digital currency, when other forms crashed, also failed. The introduction of a wearable biometric device that monitored your health, but also gathered your security risk and status, failed. For most of the planet, the societal collapse was complete.

With employment scarce, there was little in the way of taxes to be collected. No money to pay for services of course meant no police force, no fire department, no health service and, no public transport. The only transport available was used by the few volunteer civil servants that serviced the housing blocks. This transport was unreliable too as the electric cars, now the only type to exist had to rely on a very unpredictable national power grid. Wind farms and solar panels were at the mercy of extreme weather, so most times, they could not provide enough electricity to charge these few remaining vehicles.

The majority of people that did survive moved to rural areas where they were able to grow a few meagre crops to support themselves. The barter system surfaced once again, replacing currency. And old people like me were transferred to central blocks of housing, where we had some minimal form of protection and help, as crime became epidemic. Once tight communities no longer existed. We were now living in a 'dog eat dog' world.

Amazingly, considering the apocalyptic situation we now found ourselves in, there were still large, once-powerful countries run by dictators, plus a few small ones, ready to start international wars. Some were even using nuclear weapons, in misguided and desperate attempts, to survive. Not only was this wanton destruction of more human life, but also resulted in vast amounts of land made uninhabitable for thousands of years to come.

Two of these warlike nations were so vast that their population only inhabited a comparatively small portion of their country anyway. I have never been able to comprehend the insane desire to continually expand your countries borders when you had more land than you could ever possibly need. Yet still, we ploughed on.

For a brief period, there was a renewed belief in religion. Desperate for help, people prayed to gods of various faiths. But, when no relief came, only a minority of fanatics continued to believe that God would return to save us.

I know that I have not recorded all I should, but my memory is not as sharp as it used to be. Still, I hope I have written enough for you to consider. I will finish writing for now as I have to pack my few belongings in preparation for my move.

However, I will leave you with my final thoughts.

Race, religion and the colour of your skin should not separate us. We are all the same species. We should all care about each other. We are each other's caretakers, and the caretakers of this planet we were given. I cannot remember where I heard this phrase, maybe from an old song? But, now it has a more appropriate meaning to me than when I first heard it, 'united we stand, divided we fall.' Unite, grow stronger, love one another, and for God's sake, learn from our mistakes, mine included.

After my family leave tomorrow and I am relocated to my new home, I will continue to write more for histories sake. I think I need a heading for part two of the journal. Maybe I should call it, 'And yet we ploughed on!'

*Judge's Comments: If you want to see what your future holds in the next 50 years then read this short story. It made me shudder as I realised how close we are to the reality of what has been written. A story that is so unexpected.*

# PANDEMIC PICNIC

# MAUREEN EDWARDS

## Genre – Chick Lit

Why was the theme song from *Raiders of the Lost Arc* going over and over in her head? Felicia Montross hummed the tune, hoping for the best as she approached her colleagues, in person for the first time since March. Her heart raced with every step. She wore her Yankee poncho over her petit frame with a matching baseball cap covering her overgrown, grey-rooted, brunette locks. Due to COVID restrictions, the Hamilton Board of Education had decided to have their end-of-year picnic in the park, come rain or shine. Well, thanks to Tropical Storm Grace, they had got the rain.

Wearing a Mets poncho, matching hat, and mask, tall, portly Barry Lopez approached her. "So happy to see you in person! You saved my ass all year with that damn Zoom classroom."

Felicia rolled her eyes, standing six feet apart. "No worries. My daughter helped me every step of the way with all the technological questions." They walked together toward the covered section of the park, where the staff was milling around, soaked to the bone.

Barry laughed like Santa, "Ho, ho, ho! This is my son's gear. I own nothing that would have kept me dry today. My glasses are useless too. Can it possibly get any worse?" He squinted as Principal DeRosa, wearing a Hamilton hat, mask, and sweatshirt, used a bullhorn to corral everyone together.

Felicia sighed, rubbing her cold, damp hands together. "It's terrific to see everyone!" She waved to her many friends, barely recognizable with their masks on. "Well, see you later," she said, trying to lose Barry fast, as she slipped closer to the front.

Principal DeRosa said, "Hello! Welcome back, everyone! Sorry, the weather is not cooperating, but we wanted everyone together before the summer started, mainly to thank you all for your hard work. Virtual teaching was no easy task! Thanks to the PTA, they have set up a little fun scavenger hunt for you. As you know, Hamilton town has over 100 restaurants that have been closed for dining due to the pandemic. You and a partner have 30 minutes to go to as many restaurants as possible and get a token for the raffle prizes, all donated by the PTA. The grand prize will be a take-out four-course dinner, alcohol included, for the pair that gets the most tokens." The teachers cheered. "Yes, I did say alcohol is included. Check your phones for the name of your partner. When I blow the horn, you're off!"

As Felicia's phone buzzed, she prayed for a fit and active partner, like the gym teacher who ran marathons. Her stomach dropped the minute she heard Barry say, "Hey partner. What's the game plan? Stay together or split apart?" His smile was spread across his face from ear to ear.

Felicia gulped. She noticed Barry was out of breath as he waddled up to her. Upon closer look, she saw toothpaste on the corner of his chin, pointing it out so he could wipe it away.

His soft, sweet eyes watched her. "Gee, thanks." His face lit up. "I know I'm the dud of the pair, but I'll do whatever you want."

Felicia looked around, whispering, "How about you take the closest blocks, and I'll take uptown. I've been running every day, so we'll do the best we can." She shrugged her shoulders. "How about we text each other along the way, sound good?"

Suddenly the horn blew loudly and the staff scattered in all directions into the drizzle, at different paces.

Felicia began her jog along the block, then block after block. She grabbed tokens along the way from the bags on the door handles of each restaurant, dropping them into her pocket. Peeking at her phone, she was disheartened to see no update from Barry. She continued running, faster and faster, as she was sure he would not be getting very far. As she went along she passed other teachers walking, jogging, and even driving. Finally, rushing back to Hamilton Park with just seconds to spare, she saw Barry chatting and sipping coffee with Principal DeRosa. She cursed him under her breath.

Approached Felicia, Barry smiled. "Hey partner, how'd you do?"

Leaning over, gasping for air, she emptied her pockets onto the ground. Barry counted the tokens, as she said, "I think I did pretty well, and you?"

"20! You did awesomely!" Barry dumped out a garbage bag of tokens onto the pile.

Felicia's mouth dropped. She bent down to count all the tokens again. "53? How the hell did you do that?" She jumped up and down. "That's amazing!"

Blushing, he grinned. "I used my scooter. She *didn't say* we couldn't. I have a bum knee, and it kinda makes me feel cool to *zip* around on it!"

Principal DeRosa honked the bullhorn. "Shout out totals, please?" Teachers started screaming out a variety of numbers.

Felicia bowed towards Barry, giggling, "You announce it. It's all you!"

"73!" Barry waved his hands.

"Wow! Does anyone have more than 73?" Principal DeRosa looked around. It was so quiet the raindrops were the only noise.

"Barry and Felicia with 73 tokens! Congratulations, you win the grand prize! Now everyone bring in your tokens, and we'll raffle the rest of the restaurant gift certificates and email you. Thank you for all your amazing hard work this year! The kids are lucky to have you! Help yourself to some food boxes before you head out, and have a safe summer!"

Barry walked Felicia to her car. "I am so happy we won, and if I win anything else, it's yours, Felicia. I couldn't have made it through the year without you."

Felicia tilted her head. "That is so sweet, but how about we share. We are a great team! If you and I can win this scavenger hunt, anyone can do anything."

Barry's eyes welled up, "Well then, that sounds perfect to me. Better go home and dry off. Bye, Felicia."

Felicia grinned as she watched Barry hobble to the scooter and putter away into the foggy downpour.

*Judge's Comment: This is a never judge a book by its cover type of story. It also shows what a bit of ingenuity can achieve for you. Nicely written piece.*

# MENTORING WRITERS 2020 WRITING COMPETITION BOOK

# THE MYSTICAL TREEHOUSE

# &

# OTHER FUN STORIES

Available at Amazon, all good bookshops

And on the following website:

**www.annbradybooks.co.uk**

# PEN & INK DESIGNS

## INDEPENDENT PUBLISHER

**www.penandinkdesigns.co.uk**

www.ingramcontent.com/pod-product-compliance
Lightning Source LLC
Chambersburg PA
CBHW070330130626
46556CB00007B/2795